Where the Lovelight Gleams

Also by Keira Andrews

Contemporary

The Spy and the Mobster's Son
Honeymoon for One
Beyond the Sea
Ends of the Earth
Arctic Fire

Lifeguards of Barking Beach
Flash Rip
Free Wind

Holiday
The Christmas Deal
The Christmas Leap
The Christmas Veto
A Baby for Christmas
Only One Bed
Merry Cherry Christmas
Santa Daddy
In Case of Emergency
Eight Nights in December
If Only in My Dreams
Where the Lovelight Gleams
Gay Romance Holiday Collection

Sports
Kiss and Cry
Reading the Signs
Cold War
The Next Competitor
Love Match
Synchronicity (free read!)

Gay Amish Romance Series
A Forbidden Rumspringa
A Clean Break
A Way Home
A Very English Christmas

Valor Duology
Valor on the Move
Test of Valor
Complete Valor Duology

Historical

Kidnapped by the Pirate
Semper Fi
The Station
Voyageurs (free read!)

Paranormal

Kick at the Darkness Trilogy
Kick at the Darkness
Fight the Tide
Defy the Future

Fantasy

Barbarian Duet
Wed to the Barbarian
The Barbarian's Vow

Where the Lovelight Gleams

BY KEIRA ANDREWS

Dedication

To Rachel and Lisa for celebrating Christmas in
July with Ryan and Cary.

Chapter One

CHEST HEAVING, RYAN slammed the door behind him and leaned against it. "I should've just kept my big mouth shut," he muttered. "He's never going to like me the way I like him. God, I'm such an idiot!"

Pounding footsteps preceded a forceful knock. Ryan waited, breath lodged in his throat.

Cary's voice rang out. "I know you're in there. Open the door! Please."

Ryan ran a hand through his hair, then took a deep breath and blew it out. Trying to appear utterly calm, he twisted the doorknob and stepped aside as Cary rushed in.

"Didn't you hear me calling?" Cary was slightly breathless, his brow furrowed.

"No." Ryan tried to smile. "Sorry. Do you need something?"

"Do I..." Cary shook his head incredulously. "What I *need* is for you to talk to me. I heard what you said to Dara."

Blood rushed to Ryan's cheeks, and he laughed, although it came out as more of a squeak. "Oh that? I was just kidding around."

"Kidding around." Cary didn't sound convinced. "So you're *not* in love with me?"

"I…" Ryan swallowed, his throat suddenly dry. "It was a joke."

"A joke." Cary stepped forward, backing him up against the closed door.

Ryan jerked his head in a nod.

Cary was now less than a foot away. He was a few inches taller, and his broad shoulders tapered down to a narrow waist, his body muscular yet lean. Short light blond hair swept up from his forehead, and his green eyes were intense as he watched Ryan. This close, Ryan could see the flecks of gold in Cary's eyes, and his heart skipped a beat. *God, he's so beautiful.*

"That's too bad, because I've been in love with you for months."

Ryan's eyes widened. "But that's…impossible."

"Shut up and kiss me."

With that, Cary closed the gap between them, taking Ryan's face in his hands as he pressed their lips together. Their mouths opened as they kissed passionately. Ryan's pulse raced, excitement skipping up his spine as he yanked Cary against him, their bodies—

"Cut!"

Cary broke the kiss and stepped back. He looked to the director. "Go again?"

The director nodded. "Good kiss. But give me a little more on the 'I heard what you said to Dara' line." She focused on Ryan. "You're playing it just right. Great trembling in your hands. Just need to get some more sweat on your brow. You're supposed to have just run from the air lock, and it's a big ship."

As the assistant director called for makeup to bring their spray bottle, the crew prepared for another take. Cary grinned at Ryan, and dimples appeared in his cheeks. "Sorry, think I slipped a little tongue in there."

Yes, you did, and God I want more. Ignoring the desire thrumming through his veins, Ryan waved it off. "That was a good take." It was their fourth, and he'd hoped it would get easier as the day went on. Instead his yearning for Cary increased each time their lips met. Despite the twenty-five bored crew members watching, when Cary kissed him, everything else faded away.

After fantasizing about being with Cary for the past year, Ryan had told himself that the reality—even if it was fictional and not *real—*

would be a huge disappointment. On-screen kissing was supposed to be awkward and uncomfortable and epically unsexy. And in Ryan's experience it always had been.

Until now.

He wasn't supposed to breathe in the citrus of Cary's aftershave and feel desire coiling in his belly. He wasn't supposed to notice how thick Cary's eyelashes were, and how the gold in his eyes matched his hair. His knees weren't supposed to go weak because Cary's kisses were warm and wet and tasted like honey and promised so much more.

"Let's just hope the network censors don't look too closely. I swear, straight couples can practically get naked on screen, but gay characters…" Cary shook his head. "Drives me nuts. Hey, did you hear anything more from that hate group who sent the nasty letters?"

"Nah. I think Tammy took care of making sure my mail is examined more closely. It's no big deal."

Cary huffed. "No big deal? You shouldn't ever have to hear that kind of garbage. You'll tell me if it happens again, right?"

"What are you going to do? Beat them up?" Ryan secretly loved Cary's protectiveness. He smiled and nudged Cary with his elbow. "Besides, now that they're finally putting Steven and Kishi together, you'll probably start getting your own hate mail."

Cary still frowned. "Yeah, but it's not the same. Everyone knows I'm not gay in real life." He scoffed. "No way a tough guy like my dad would ever have a gay son. No one would believe it even if it was true."

"Yeah." Ryan stopped himself before his brain went too far down the "what if" road. "By the way, your scales are coming loose a bit on your neck."

"Crap. I keep sweating them off."

As the makeup team sprayed fake sweat onto Ryan's forehead and touched up the purple scales crawling up the side of Cary's neck and across one cheek, Ryan breathed deeply. He reminded himself that none of it was real. Cary's declaration of love and his kiss that left Ryan buzzing—it was all for the cameras. Nothing more.

So he should stop remembering the press of Cary's body and how his firm muscles had felt beneath Ryan's hands. Ryan was in good shape himself, but he was positively ordinary next to Cary's golden handsomeness and toned, perfect body. Not too bulky, but just right. As Cary tipped his head to give the makeup artist better access to his neck, Ryan imagined kissing him there, sucking on the tender skin and—

One of the show's publicists approached, her heels clacking across the spaceship set. "How are we today, gentlemen?"

Ryan smiled. "Hey, Tammy. We're good."

"Excellent. The reporter from *Out and Proud* will be here in an hour. He wanted to see the kiss filmed, but as you know we're keeping the set closed. If anyone leaks this kiss before the episode, I will eat their lungs for breakfast."

Cary smirked. "And their balls for lunch?"

"Nope. Balls are for second breakfast." Tammy winked.

The director called out, "Places everyone."

Fake sweat artfully moistening his dark hair where it fell across his forehead, Ryan took his position to run into Steven's room once more. Part of him hoped the director would want dozens of takes, but he wasn't sure how much longer he could keep himself in check. He'd worn extra-tight briefs to keep from embarrassing himself, but his one-piece bodysuit costume didn't leave much to the imagination.

The second assistant cameraman clapped down the slate in front of the camera. "*Space Academy*, two-twelve, scene nine, take five."

Silence settled over the set, and the director yelled, "Action!"

As he ran and slammed the door once more, Ryan's heart pounded anew, and he couldn't help but look forward to Cary's next kiss.

AFTER LEAVING HIS TRAILER, Ryan almost walked straight into Tammy, who tapped a manicured nail on her watch. "You're five minutes late."

"Actually, I'm three and a half minutes late, but I had to go to the bathroom. Besides, actors are supposed to be late. And/or hungover."

Tammy laughed and tucked a red curl behind her ear. "You haven't reached that phase of your career yet. Talk to me when this show has garnered more than a cult following and you've made at least one successful slasher flick during hiatus."

Cary was already seated in a director's chair on the command deck of the set, which wasn't being used for filming that day. It was little more than a *Star Trek* rip-off, but there were only so many layouts of a spaceship that worked well for filming. Cary still wore his dark green one-piece costume, but the top half pooled around his waist, and he wore a white T-shirt.

It was a V-neck, and Ryan tried not to look at Cary's light chest hair poking out. He wondered for the hundredth time what it would be like to run his fingers through it and taste

Cary's nipples and—

Never. Going. To happen.

With a smile on his face, Ryan sat in the empty chair beside Cary and shook hands with the reporter seated across from them. Tammy lingered in the background by the space-thruster control station.

The chubby, middle-aged reporter smiled. "Hi, I'm Chuck Basilica from *Out and Proud.* Thanks for meeting with me today."

"I'm Ryan Drake. It's our pleasure," Ryan answered. He and Cary had done a ton of press for the show at the upfronts in May, and they had a system down pat. They'd alternate answering questions, share a few amusing anecdotes, and generally be their most humble, charming selves.

Of course now that their story line was heating up, the gay press was taking interest. Chuck didn't waste any time.

"Rumor has it the sexual tension between Steven and Kishi is going to move from subtext to text during February sweeps. You'll be the first gay human/alien love story on American network TV. Is this true?"

Cary answered. "Well, we're definitely exploring our characters in greater depth this season, and relationships between many of the cadets will be evolving."

"Hmm. That sounds like a yes to me." Chuck smiled.

Ryan smiled back. "All we can say is that fans should keep watching, because there's some great stuff coming up for Steven and Kishi."

"Fair enough. Now, were you both surprised at how quickly fans embraced your characters? Individually, but especially as a potential couple. There are quite a few 'Stishi' fansites out there."

"I think we were both surprised, and of course it's an honor," Cary replied. "I mean, we were just happy our little midseason replacement show got a pickup for season two, and that viewers took to it so passionately. We may not get the highest ratings, but the fans are extremely vocal and loyal. The best in the world. We feel so blessed to be a part of *Space Academy*."

"Let's talk about your careers for a moment." Chuck glanced at his notepad. "Cary, of course you're part of a Hollywood dynasty. You were named after family friend Cary Grant, isn't that right?"

He smiled. "That's right. I only hope I can have a career half as incredible as his."

"Your father and grandfather made their mark in action and adventure movies, while you've focused more on drama and now sci-fi. Do you feel any pressure to live up to their legacy?"

Cary's smile didn't falter, but Ryan noticed the way Cary's jaw flexed briefly, his shoulders tightening. "Only in the best way. I'm so proud of Dad and Grandpa, and they've always been so supportive of me."

As Cary went on about his family, telling the public what they wanted to hear, Ryan put on his best listening face. He remembered the first little cast get-together at the exec producer's house one night in the Hollywood Hills. Ryan had gone outside to get some air and stumbled across Cary on the phone with his father.

"But, Dad, it's a good show. Plenty of movie actors are doing TV now. It's not the way it was before. It's a great part! I want to do it. Besides, I can't exactly turn down steady work."

Cary paused, and Ryan could hear Robert Holloway's raised voice through the phone but couldn't make out what he was saying.

Cary went on, "I want to make my own way. I can have a good career in TV. Maybe do some theater in the summers. I think it's worth a shot." He paused again. "Well, I'm sorry you feel that way, but I guess you're used to disappointment by now, aren't you?"

Ryan tried to back away without being heard but of course promptly tripped on the leg of a deck chair, sending it clattering.

Cary whirled. "Dad, I've gotta go." He hung up and eyed Ryan cautiously. "Hey. Look, if you could just forget you heard any of that…"

"Heard what?" Ryan raised his hands. "I didn't hear a thing."

The tension in Cary's face relaxed. "Thanks, man. Ryan, right? I think we have a couple of scenes together in the pilot."

"Yeah, we do. You want to run lines this weekend?"

Cary smiled, his eyes crinkling. "Absolutely."

Now, almost two years after they met, Cary was just about Ryan's favorite person in the world. Of course Cary was straight, and they'd never be anything more than friends. Which was totally fine with Ryan. Well, not *totally* fine. But he was working on it.

"And let's talk about *your* background, Ryan. You're from Toronto. How has it been adjusting to life in La-La Land?"

"I've lived here for a few years now. There are always great things about any city, and LA has so much to offer. It was a bit of a culture shock, but being close to the beach sure helps."

"You came out while you were still in Toronto performing in a local production of *Rent.* You mentioned having lunch with your boyfriend in an interview, and when *Space*

Academy premiered, many bloggers and gossip sites picked up on the old article. Do you regret coming out so early in your career? Do you think you'll get pigeonholed?"

He'd expected the question, so Ryan resisted the urge to sigh long-sufferingly. He wished it didn't come up in every interview. "No, I don't regret it at all. I've been out since my senior year of high school. It's just who I am, and I don't think it's impacted my career negatively. I played a straight character in a movie during summer hiatus." He shrugged. "All I can do is give the best performances I can and hope to continue to have opportunities."

Cary interjected, his tone firm. "I think Ryan is an inspiration to other gay actors. And straight actors, for that matter. Someone's sexuality shouldn't matter in this day and age. He's an amazing artist and person."

Warmth bloomed in Ryan's chest. "I'm lucky that Cary and everyone here at *Space Academy* are completely supportive. I hope that we'll get to the point one day when it won't be a big deal anymore."

"I hope so too," Chuck replied. "So are you seeing anyone, Ryan?"

"No, there's no one special right now." *No one I can actually date, that is.*

"Cary, you've been seeing *Succubus High* star

Amanda Walker for over a year now. Any wedding bells in the future?"

Cary chuckled. "We'll have to see. Amanda's a great girl."

Actually, Amanda's a high-maintenance pain in the ass. Ryan kept a pleasant expression on his face. It wasn't that he was jealous or anything. Okay, maybe he was. But Cary deserved so much more than her. He reminded himself that it wasn't as if Amanda Walker was the only thing standing between him and Cary. She was irrelevant. Cary was straight. The end.

"You guys are both twenty-five now. How does it feel to be playing high school students?"

Ryan chuckled. "Well, I don't think we're the oldest actors to play teenagers."

"With his big brown doe eyes and baby face, I think he'll be playing a high schooler for at least five more years." Cary laughed, eyes crinkling.

"But we love our roles," Ryan added. "High school—whether here on Earth or orbiting the fifth moon of the newly discovered planet Alida—is so rife with drama and potential for character growth."

Chuck's eyebrow popped up. "Ah yes. Such as discovering one's sexuality?"

Cary and Ryan shared a glance and a smile. Cary answered. "That is a common theme,

Chuck. I think our fans are really going to enjoy our characters' arcs as this season continues in the new year."

Tammy cleared her throat. "I'm afraid we have to end things there. Ryan and Cary are needed back on set."

They said good-bye to Chuck, and Ryan checked his call sheet. The next scene was an "intimate moment" between Steven and Kishi. No kiss, but they'd both be shirtless and playing a particularly close game of *imperia*, a basketball-ish game. The scene was early in the episode, before their kiss, and Steven would be barely able to contain his attraction to Kishi.

Ryan took a fortifying breath as he headed back to set. He didn't think of himself as a Method actor, but he was certainly living and breathing his character's emotions these days.

WITH A SIGH, Ryan popped open a can of soda as he sat back on the couch in his trailer. He still had one more scene to shoot, and it was going to be a long day. As he picked up the TV remote, there was a knock on the door.

His heart stupidly skipped a beat when he found Cary waiting outside. "Hey, man! I'm wrapped. Just wanted to say merry Christmas and all that."

Ryan ushered him in and handed him a bottle of water from the fridge since Cary didn't drink soda. That was just one of the reasons he'd been featured on the cover of *Men's Health* and Ryan never would be. Ryan worked out and kept trim and healthy, but he wasn't a heartthrob like Cary.

"Big plans for the holidays?" Ryan asked. "Will you be with your mom or dad?"

"Neither. Dad's in Thailand shooting another sequel to *Blowing Shit Up*."

Ryan laughed. "Is this *Strike Back* part four?"

"Yep. The world's appetite for explosions and cheap one-liners continues unabated." He flopped down on the couch. "Besides, my stepmother's with him, and I can't deal with her. She seriously tried to give me parental advice at Thanksgiving."

Ryan sat beside Cary and swung his feet up onto the low coffee table. Most movie stars would sniff at his small oak-paneled trailer, but with a sofa bed, shower, toilet, and kitchenette, the twelve-foot space was luxury for Ryan. He still wasn't used to being waited on, and at first the trailer had seemed unnecessary. But for the long days of shooting, he was very glad to have it.

"Tell me you're exaggerating."

Cary took a swig of water. "I wish. No, it seems that in Janelle's twenty impressive years here on Earth, she's learned a lot. She was quite put out that I didn't want the benefit of her extensive knowledge when picking my hiatus project."

"Wow. Okay, so what's your mom doing for Christmas?"

"She'll be in Hawaii. I'd go, but Amanda booked us into a spa for a cleanse."

"A cleanse? For *Christmas*?"

Cary grimaced. "Yeah, nothing but lettuce and lemon water or something. Oh and pepper or hot sauce, I think. Yum. It's in the desert near Palm Springs. Lots of yoga and massage, at least."

"And *starvation*. No turkey? No stuffing? No cookies? It's just not Christmas without a ton of fattening food."

"Eh, it's no big deal." Cary shrugged. "I've never really had a real Christmas. Growing up, my parents were always getting married and divorced, and they vacationed in the tropics. A white Christmas and the family all together is just something I saw on TV."

Ryan's jaw dropped. "You've never had snow at Christmas?" He realized he was practically shouting and flushed at his overreaction. "Sorry. Christmas has always been my favorite holiday."

"The most wonderful time of the year? Well, you're Canadian, so it's understandable," Cary replied playfully. His smile faded. "Nah, Christmas was just never a big deal. I got presents and everything, but it's never been a big special day with walking in a winter wonderland and all that."

"I'm sorry." Cary seemed uncharacteristically melancholy about it. "Hey, you're more than welcome to join me and my family in the Great White North."

To Ryan's surprise, Cary's face lit up. "Really?"

The invite had slipped out, and he hadn't really been serious, but the thought of actually spending Christmas with Cary had Ryan's stomach flip-flopping. "Of course. I'm flying home tomorrow, and we're going up to our cottage on Friday. More snow than you can shake a stick at." He knew he should limit the time he spent with Cary off set, but... *But I can still look even if I can't touch.*

Again, Cary's smile disappeared, and he slumped back against the cushions. "Man, I wish I could, but Amanda will kill me if I try to back out of the spa. Besides, I wouldn't want to intrude on you and your family."

"It wouldn't be an intrusion at all. My parents keep saying they want to meet you. You're my best friend out here."

Cary's expression was unreadable. Pleased, maybe? "Really? Thanks, man. That's nice to hear. You know you're my boy too." He punched Ryan's shoulder lightly.

Ryan cleared his throat and pretended his whole body wasn't on fire. "Well, the invitation stands if you change your mind."

They smiled awkwardly at each other. Things had always been totally comfortable between them, but now that they'd kissed on set, Ryan felt on edge. If he relaxed, he was afraid he'd do something that would cross the boundaries without even thinking about it. Now any kind of touch barring a shoulder punch seemed too intimate. *He's not your boyfriend. It's all pretend.*

Their eyes met, and Ryan swore a current surged between them, shooting up his spine and then right down to his dick. Cary licked his lips, and they stared at each other in the silence. Ryan could feel the heat from Cary's body beside him on the couch, and Cary seemed to be leaning into him.

A soft knock on the door was followed by a PA calling out, "Ryan? We're ready for you."

The strange mood broken, Cary drained his bottle. "See ya next year." He stood, then pulled

Ryan up into a straight-guy hug, slapping his back with a thump.

"Right, see you next year. Merry Christmas."

As he walked to set, Ryan decided it was a good thing they had three weeks until they had to be back in the second week of January. Time to get this crush on Cary under control. Between work and their friendship, they had a good thing going, and Ryan was damned if he was going to mess that up.

Chapter Two

RYAN'S CELL BUZZED on the seat beside him as he pulled off the highway into Parry Sound's mall—which was more of a glorified plaza. He scanned the busy lot for a parking space and glanced at the display. His stomach somersaulted ridiculously, and he quickly pulled into a spot by the huge snowbank created by the snow plows at the edge of the lot.

He swiped his finger across the screen. "Hello?"

"Hey, man. It's Cary."

"Hi." *Say something!* "Um, what's up? Everything okay?"

"I kind of did something a little impulsive."

"Okay. What did you do?"

"I'm at Pearson right now."

Ryan blinked. The cold must have blocked his ears. "Pearson? Airport? In Toronto?"

"That's the one. I've been trying to get a hold of you for two days, but you never picked up."

"Shit, sorry. There's no service out on the bay." Ryan's heart thumped. *Cary's here.*

"You said the invite stood and some stuff happened and I really needed to get away. But you were probably just being polite, being Canadian and all, so I'll just catch the next flight home and—"

"No!" Ryan cleared his throat and took a breath. "Of course you're still welcome. I can come pick you up, but it'll take me about two hours to drive down to the airport." He checked his watch. They'd miss dinner, but shouldn't be back too late.

Cary chuckled. "Dude, I'm renting a car. Don't even think about driving back down here."

"But the roads are slippery. You're not used to the snow."

"I'll be fine. I went four-wheeling in Aspen once. Just give me the address and I'll GPS it."

Palms tingling, Ryan gave Cary instructions on how to reach his family's cottage on Georgian Bay, since there wasn't a street address. It was an hour outside of the booming metropolis of Parry Sound (population 6,191) on country roads that would be dark before too long. "Use your brights once you get off highway sixty-nine. Unless it's snowing and there's a whiteout, because the brights will just make it worse."

"I'll be fine, Ry. Don't worry, the California boy will go slowly."

"Let me give you the number for the cottage in case you get delayed. We have a landline."

When Cary had all the details Ryan could think of, they said good-bye and hung up. After pulling out his mom's shopping list, Ryan hurried toward the grocery store, his boots crunching on the salt in the parking lot. As he walked through the sliding doors, he caught a glimpse of his reflection and realized he was grinning like a fool, but he couldn't help himself.

"WHY DIDN'T YOU tell me sooner you were inviting a guest?"

Ryan's mom, Maureen, glared at him with hands on hips. Her glasses had slipped down her nose, and flour dusted her cheek. Her dark hair was starting to go gray, and with a festive red-and-green apron on over her plump form, she resembled Mrs. Claus just a bit. Her English West Country accent always came out more when she was agitated. "I've only made a casserole for supper!"

"Because I didn't know. I didn't think he'd actually come, but his plans fell through." Ryan hadn't allowed himself to speculate too much about what might have happened and what it meant for Amanda and Cary's relationship. "And a casserole is fine, Mom."

"Look at this place! You're helping me clean up, young man."

Gazing around at the tidy kitchen, Ryan's eyebrows shot up. "Oh yeah, Mom. It's a real pigsty."

"Go straighten up the living room. What does he like to eat? Is he one of those vegantarians?"

"It's just vegan, and no. He eats meat. You don't have to make anything special."

Leaving behind his grumbling mother, Ryan straightened up the wood pile by the large stone fireplace that dominated one wall of the living room. The cottage was an A-frame, narrowing at the top to a point, built with stone and wood and furnished in a style he thought of as "comfy country." Not fashionable by any means, but warm and welcoming, with a thick rug by the hearth on the wood floor and a soft couch against the opposite wall. Two armchairs and a love seat framed the couch and a wagon-wheel coffee table.

The main floor was decked out for the holidays, with garlands and wreaths and stockings hung by the chimney with care. The only thing missing was the Christmas tree, which Ryan was going to cut down the next day, December 23. He wasn't sure why it was family tradition to get the tree each year on that date, but it was.

Ethan and Amy zoomed by him on their way from upstairs to the kitchen. "I still don't get why there's no cable here," Ethan groused.

At eight and six, Ryan's nephew and niece already owned more technological gadgets than Ryan did, yet it never seemed to be enough. But Ryan remembered his own complaints as a kid. Ethan and Amy were both dark haired and round faced—the spitting image of Lisa, and therefore Ryan as well. They always joked that Ryan could kidnap them and pass them off as his own.

"I'm boooooored!" Amy whined. "Can't we watch a movie?"

"Oh yes, it's a hard life, I know," Maureen replied. "You get one movie a day and you've used your allowance already. The cottage is for family time. You little devils spend enough time glued to your phones and TVs and computers. And if you're bored, I'll find you some work to do! Or I'll have to tell Santa you've been naughty."

As the kids continued to whine in the kitchen, pestering their grandmother for shortbread cookies, Ryan's sister came downstairs with a duster in hand. She pulled her long brown hair up into a ponytail and smiled slyly. "I hear there's a guest coming."

Avoiding Lisa's gaze, Ryan put another log on the fire. "Yeah, my friend Cary. From the show."

With a glance to the kitchen, where their mom was giving the kids jobs as her helpers, Lisa whispered, "I know exactly who Cary is, little brother. You guys did the kissing scene last week, hmm?"

"What? How did you know that?"

She rolled her eyes. "There's this thing called the Internet. A reliable source told TMZ that—"

"Ugh, I've heard enough. And Lisa, we're just friends."

"*Uh-huh.* But you want more."

Marching to the cupboard to pull out the vacuum, Ryan scoffed. "Why would you say that? He's straight."

"Why would I say that? Because you've been mooning over him for over a year! You may be an award-winning actor, but you're not fooling me."

Ryan rolled his eyes. "I'm not an award-winning actor."

"Teen Choice awards totally count, little brother. Even if it's for Cutest TV Heartthrob. You beat out some stiff competition for that title."

Barking out a laugh, Ryan jammed the vacuum plug into the wall and pulled out the cord. "We're friends. The end." He stepped on the button on the back of the vacuum, and it roared to life.

Lisa stepped close, still keeping her voice low. "He's going to have to share your room, you know."

Ryan swallowed hard. "There are two beds up there. It's no big deal."

"Sure. No big deal."

"Lisa, please. Just…don't."

She dropped her teasing tone. "I'm sorry. I promise I won't embarrass you in front of your friend. It's just that I've had years of practice, and it's a hard habit to break." She leaned up and pressed a kiss to his cheek.

Although she was five years older, Ryan had been taller since he was thirteen, much to Lisa's chagrin. He gave her shoulder a knock. "Okay, squirt."

"Hilarious. Come on, let's get this place clean—well, clean*er*—while Mom keeps those two busy."

"Where are Dad and Tony?"

Lisa rolled her eyes. "Ice fishing. Where else?"

Ryan chuckled as he vacuumed the rug. Lisa's husband Tony and their father were two peas in pod when it came to fishing. "It was good of you to marry the son Dad always wanted."

"Bite your tongue, Ryan Patrick Drake!" his mother yelled back from the kitchen.

"Mom, I'm kidding!"

Ryan and Lisa shared a glance and burst out laughing. Lisa tugged on her earlobes, their old signal from childhood that their mom was listening. *Ears of a hawk*, Lisa mouthed, and they both chortled.

"What's so funny?" Their mom stuck her head out of the kitchen doorway.

Dissolving into giggles, Ryan and Lisa went back to their tasks. When they were finished, Ryan went up to his room to make sure it was neat and ready for Cary's arrival in—he checked his watch for the umpteenth time—forty-three minutes. Give or take.

The second floor housed his parents' master bedroom, two guest rooms, and the cottage's main bathroom with tub. There was a small toilet on the main floor, but everyone had to take turns showering on the second floor. Ryan clambered up the ladder to the third floor loft, which had been his room since he was a kid.

The ladder led into the middle of the room, which was the top of the A-frame structure. There was just enough room to stand along the center of the narrow room, with the walls slanting in on either side. To the left of the ladder was Ryan's single bed and small dresser under the window at the end of the room. There was a window on the other side as well, and an identical single bed and dresser.

When they were little, the bed to the right of the stairs had been Lisa's, until she turned twelve and deemed herself too mature to share a room with her little brother. Over the years cousins and friends had slept there. *Now it would be Cary.* Going over to his bed, Ryan flopped down, gazing at the familiar slanted walls and the old space-themed wallpaper. When it got dark, the glow-in-the-dark solar system stickers would appear.

Even though he made a very good salary now, his parents had refused his offer to renovate the old cottage. His father, Jack, had simply furrowed his brow at the idea, while Maureen had fluttered her hands and told him to save his money, because God knew an actor's income was never steady and *Space Academy* could be cancelled at any moment.

Ryan smiled to himself. No matter how many teenage girls put his face up in their lockers, his family always treated him as same old Ryan. At least they had let him pay for a new deck overlooking the expanse of Georgian Bay.

He just hoped Cary wouldn't feel too out of place. He grew up in mansions, and an old single bed in a cottage would be way outside his comfort zone. Not to mention Ryan's comfort zone. Sometimes he'd get hard just *looking* at Cary, let alone sharing a room with him. Seeing him undress. Hearing him breathing, knowing he was only feet away…

Groaning, Ryan stood. He needed a cold shower, but going out to the shed for more firewood would do the trick. He checked his watch. *Thirty-seven minutes.*

BY THE TIME CARY was seventy-four minutes late, Ryan thought he might vomit. Snow was falling, and clouds obscured the moon and stars. The snow wasn't heavy, but the roads would be slick, and Cary wasn't even used to much rain in LA, and—

"You're going to wear the carpet out." His mother handed Ryan a hot mug of tea. "He still had to rent a car, and if he's driving slowly, he's bound to take a bit longer than usual. He might have stopped for coffee along the way."

"I know, I know. But…he's not used to snow. Winter driving can be dangerous."

She patted his cheek. "Aren't you sweet to be so concerned about your chum."

As if on cue, footsteps thumped on the porch. Ryan raced to the door and threw it open. He sighed. "Oh."

His father's laugh boomed through the cottage from the small mudroom where they kept their boots and snow shovels. It wasn't insulated but helped keep out the cold from the main building when people were coming and going in the winter months. "That's a fine greeting from my only son." He held up a cooler. "We caught an even dozen, Mo."

Maureen took the cooler, laughing and squirming away as Jack tickled her. "Get those cold hands away from me!"

Tony followed and unzipped his coat. "Everything okay, Ryan?"

"Huh?" Ryan realized he must have been frowning. "Yeah, fine. My friend's late."

"Your friend?" Tony stooped so he didn't bang his head passing through the doorway. At six-five, he often had to watch where he was walking.

"Cary. From work."

"The cute one?"

Lisa cleared her throat from the couch, where she was supervising the kids' game of Candyland. Her eyes twinkled. "Should I be jealous?"

Rolling his eyes, Tony kissed his children and then planted a big one on his wife. "Babe, you know I don't swing that way." He glanced apologetically at Ryan. "Not that there's anything wrong with that."

Ryan laughed. "Let me guess. Maria's a fan?" Tony's teenage sister was always glued to Ryan's side at family gatherings, asking him a million and one questions about Hollywood. He tried to tell her it wasn't as glamorous as it seemed, but she was unconvinced.

"Think I can get an autograph for her? She's going to be so jealous when she finds out I spent Christmas with not one, but *two* TV stars."

Ryan glanced at his watch again. "Yeah. Sure."

He heard Tony ask Lisa, "What's up with him?" but Ryan didn't hear her response as he raced to the window. He could hear a vehicle approaching, and headlights flashed past as a large SUV pulled up.

Ryan took a couple of deep breaths as he put on his coat. Still his stomach clenched, and he was a pile of jittery nerves.

It's the same old Cary. Your straight friend. Get a grip.

In the mudroom, he yanked on his boots and then hopped down the few steps to the ground, closing the glass storm door behind him. He waved and approached Cary's rental. Cary killed the engine and opened the SUV door. "Is this a good spot to park?"

"Yeah, it's fine. Did you find the place okay?"

Cary got out and pulled Ryan into one of his patented back-slapping hugs. "Yep, your directions were good. Just took me a while to get out of the airport. Realized I'd better not show up at Christmas empty-handed, so I hit up the airport stores." He stepped back and spread his arms, displaying his hooded black parka. "Also bought my first winter coat. And Jesus, do I need it!" He shivered.

Ryan grinned. "You're not in Kansas any-more, Toto."

"So that makes you Dorothy, huh?" Cary elbowed him playfully. "Can you help me with this stuff?" He opened the back of the SUV.

"Holy crap! Did you buy out the entire airport?" There were at least a dozen shopping bags.

"Well, I wasn't sure exactly who was here, so I got a variety of gifts for different ages and stuff."

"You really didn't have to do that." Ryan's heart sank. "We don't have anything for you."

"Are you kidding? Letting me spend Christmas here is more than enough." He peered around at the snow-topped trees. "It's beautiful. Like something out of a movie."

"Boys! Dinner's almost ready!" Maureen's voice rang out from the mudroom door.

Ryan picked up as many bags as he could carry. "Okay, I guess you'd better meet the family. They can be a bit much when they all get going. And once we get into the eggnog, there's no telling how things'll turn out."

Cary grinned. "Sounds perfect." He reached out and squeezed Ryan's shoulder. "Thanks again for inviting me. You're...a great friend."

Ryan tried to ignore the sparks of desire he felt at Cary's touch, even through the layers of fabric. "Anytime." Snowflakes caught in Cary's thick eyelashes, and Ryan tightened his grip on the shopping bags, resisting the urge to brush the flakes away.

After they took off their boots in the mud-room, Ryan's mother ushered them inside. In the doorway, she drew a startled Cary into a hug. "Welcome! So lovely to have you, Cary."

"I...thank you, Mrs. Drake." Cary smiled.

She pressed a kiss to his cheek and pointed

up at the bough of leaves and berries hanging above the door. "Mistletoe."

Ryan shrugged apologetically. "It's tradition."

Cary's eyes crinkled, and he gazed up. "That's awesome. I've only ever seen it in movies."

"You'd better come in, or I'll have to kiss you too." The words were out of his mouth before Ryan could stop himself. He stuttered. "I…um, here, let me get your coat."

Jesus, get a grip! Even joking about kissing Cary was a bad idea. He just hoped he wouldn't do something stupid and ruin their friendship by New Year's.

AS LISA SCURRIED around on her hands and knees, sniffing the corners of the living room, they all roared with laughter. She wiggled her nose and stuck her teeth out over her bottom lip.

"Bugs Bunny?" Tony asked.

Lisa glared as the sands in the timer ran out. "Rat race! That was a rat!"

"Ohhhh. Mom, that was smart," Amy said.

Pushing herself up onto her feet, Lisa laughed. "Thank you, sweetie. Too bad my team didn't think so!" She sat back on the couch next to Cary, shaking her head in mock sadness. "You'd think an actor would be better at this game."

"Hey, did I not act out *March of the Penguins* perfectly?"

"Okay, I'll give you that. The rest of you, get it together!"

They were divided into two teams, sitting across from each other with the wagon wheel coffee table between them. Ryan passed Amy the dice. "Roll a six, okay?"

Remarkably, she did, and she and Ryan high-fived. It was Jack's turn to perform, and he had to hum a song for their team to guess. Jack read the card, and his eyebrows disappeared into his hairline. "What's a Feist?"

"She's a singer, Dad," Lisa answered. "You won't know any of her songs, so take another card."

This one he did know, and as his dad hummed "I Wanna Hold Your Hand," Ryan glanced around happily. He'd had a few glasses of spiked nog—along with wine at dinner—and a pleasant warmth suffused his chest. His family had welcomed Cary enthusiastically, and Cary had fit right in, joking around and getting in on the family's playful bickering. As the evening wore on, Ryan couldn't remember the last time he'd felt so relaxed. So peaceful.

His mother quickly guessed the song, and then it was her turn to act out a clue. They all howled with laughter as she beat her chest and dragged her knuckles before swooning with a goofy smile on her face. "Monkey love!" Ryan called out.

His team won the game a little after ten o'clock, and they called it a night. As Ryan led Cary up to their room, his pulse increased. At the top of the stairs, he waved his arm grandly. "Welcome to the little-known Canadian cousin of the Ritz Carlton. Sumptuous comfort awaits."

"This is so cool." Cary gazed around the room, a smile dimpling his cheeks. "I can just picture you here as a kid. It must be nice, having everything be the same. I grew up on movie sets more than anywhere else. Hotel rooms."

Ryan had brought up Cary's things earlier and placed them by the spare bed. Cary sat down on it, and the mattress creaked.

Ryan grimaced. "That mattress is years old. I hope it'll be okay."

"It's perfect, Ry." Cary grinned. "I'll just climb in with you if this bed isn't comfy enough."

Ryan's laugh was slightly manic. "Yeah, plenty of room over here." *Ha-ha.* "So the bathroom's on the second floor. There's a night-light down there, but be careful going down the ladder. When you're half-asleep you can end up on your ass."

"Will do." Cary stood and unzipped his small suitcase. "I usually sleep in the nude, but I guess I'll freeze my tail off if I do that." He pulled out a T-shirt and flannel pajama bottoms.

At the thought of Cary naked, Ryan turned away, desire shivering over his skin. "Yeah, gets a little cold up here." Keeping his back turned, Ryan quickly pulled on his pajamas.

Cary chuckled. "Are those…Christmas pajamas?"

Wait, did Cary just watch me undress? Ryan turned and held up his hands. "Guilty as charged. Santa brought them for me last year."

"Santa. As in, Claus?"

"Yeah, every year my mom gets us presents from Santa. Just silly stuff." He glanced down. "Like reindeer pajamas."

"Love 'em." Cary climbed into bed. "I think it's really cool that your family's so into Christmas and everything. It's nice."

"I never really thought about it. But yeah, it is." Ryan flicked off the overhead light and got into bed. As darkness settled in, the solar system stuck to the slanted ceiling above his bed glowed faintly. Ryan cleared his throat. "So…is everything okay with Amanda?"

There was only silence for a moment, and he thought Cary might have gone to sleep already.

"It's over. It just wasn't working out. We were fighting all the time."

Ryan tried to keep his voice somber despite the giddy whirl of joy whipping through him. "I'm sorry to hear it."

"Are you?"

Ryan's heart skipped a beat. Cary was across the room in the dark, and they couldn't see each other, which was a good thing since Ryan probably looked guilty as hell. "Of course!"

"Dude, it's cool. You and Amanda just never seemed to click."

"No. I guess not. But I'm still sorry. I know you cared about her."

"Yeah. I guess. We're just not right for each other. Wanna hear something crazy?" He paused. "I think she was jealous of you."

Ryan swallowed hard. "Of me?" He and Amanda had certainly never been friends, and he'd often felt the sharp edges of her piercing gaze when she visited the set. "That's definitely crazy. We work together. We're friends."

"She kept trying to convince me to quit the show. Never mind that I have a contract. She thinks our story line will hurt my career."

"Oh." Ryan couldn't help the stab of hurt. "But everyone knows you're straight. It'll be fine."

There was a long moment of silence. "Yeah. Anyway. Thanks for letting me crash your Christmas. 'Night."

Clearly Cary didn't want to talk about it any further. "'Night."

Silence descended, and Ryan closed his eyes. It was strange to be sharing a room with Cary—especially *this* room. It felt as if there was something hanging in the air, but he wasn't sure what. After a while, Cary's breathing evened out, and Ryan burrowed deeply under the covers and drifted away. Visions of Cary danced in his head, with not a sugarplum in sight.

Chapter Three

"SO HOW DOES THIS work?"

Ryan turned off their laneway onto Shell Bay Road. It hadn't been freshly plowed yet, but his father's pickup could manage the new inches of snow. "Well, first there's a seedling, and it grows in the earth and—"

"Ha-ha." Cary rolled his eyes. "I mean how does it work to cut down a Christmas tree? Can you just walk into the woods?"

"I guess you could, but there's a tree farm not too far away." The sun blinked out from behind a cloud, and Ryan adjusted the shade.

Cary squinted. "Man, it's brighter than the beach with all this snow. It's nice, though."

"Especially when you don't have to shovel it. One of the best parts of Lisa having kids is that they get to do all our old chores." He cleared his throat. "Uh, not that I don't love the kids."

"Of course. Slave labor's just a bonus."

"Exactly."

They laughed, and before long Ryan turned onto a winding road cutting through the forest. Fortunately it had been plowed, but he still went slowly. The sun was mostly blocked by the tall trees, lending the area a slightly mysterious air. Ryan spotted movement on the left and took his foot off the gas. As the truck rounded a bend, dozens of eyes swiveled toward them in unison.

Cary gasped softly. "Wow. What are they all doing here?"

Ryan pulled over and shut off the engine. The deer all stood motionless, watching. "It's a feeding station. Must be because there's so much snow this year. Sometimes the local anglers and hunters group will feed them if they're getting too hungry. With global warming everything's all topsy-turvy."

"Wait, the hunters feed them? Aren't they just going to kill them?" Cary glanced around as if expecting men with guns to materialize from the forest.

"Not until hunting season next November. But yeah, it's kinda weird when you think about it."

"Kinda. But it's cool. I've never seen deer up close."

Ryan lowered his window, and the deer

remained frozen. But after another minute, the animals began eating again. Cary took off his seat belt and slid closer on the seat, his warm breath puffing into the cold air. Ryan shivered, but not from the chill. Cary pressed against his side, leaning close to peer out the window.

"They're beautiful," Cary whispered. "I wish we could pet them. I know we can't, though." He was silent for a moment. "I hope they're fast runners and the hunters are lousy shots."

Ryan smiled. "Me too," he whispered back.

They watched the deer for ten minutes until another truck came, this one noisier and causing the deer to bound into the protection of the forest. Ryan put the truck into drive, and Cary slid back across the seat. Even with the window shut, Ryan felt chilled and bereft on his right side where Cary had been so close a moment ago.

Half an hour later, they struggled through knee-deep snow. Ryan had an ax slung over his shoulder, and he led the way. Cary had picked up top-of-the-line boots, which was a good thing since in LA he only ever wore flip-flops or sneakers.

"How do you know where we're going?" Cary gazed around at the sea of trees. It was brighter at the tree farm, and Cary's hair gleamed golden in the sun. "They all look the same."

Ryan mock gasped. "The same? No, no. Among these trees is The One. The one true tree that I must find to bring home to my family. Usually it would be my dad accompanying me on this quest. But this year it's you who must prove your bravery, good knight."

Cary chuckled. "Are there Orcs in this forest? Because I didn't sign up for Orcs."

"You're a Portigan warrior. You can handle a few Orcs." Ryan changed course and went deeper into the trees.

"Too bad I left my warp blaster at home."

The snow crunched underfoot as they continued along, away from the families and other people looking for their own trees. The sun darted in and out of the clouds, but there was no wind, so even though it was below zero, it didn't feel cold. At least not to Ryan. Cary's cheeks were rosy in the chill.

"Are you warm enough? Here, take my toque." Ryan pulled off his woolen beanie hat and held it out.

"Your what?" Cary laughed. "It's okay, I'm fine."

"You're not used to this weather. Take it."

After a moment, Cary relented and slipped on the red hat. "Thanks. How do I look?"

Gorgeous. Perfect. Sexy as hell. "Fine." Ryan's

voice sounded strange, and he cleared his throat. "My mom's probably knitting you your own as we speak, so I hope you like it."

Cary grinned. "I love it." After a moment, he stopped walking. "See something you like?"

Heart thumping, Ryan huffed out a strangled breath. "What?"

Cary waved his arm around. "The trees. You looked like maybe you spotted one."

"Right. No. Not yet."

Ryan started walking again and hoped the blush staining his cheeks would be mistaken for a reaction to the temperature. He ducked around a particularly large pine, and then he saw it.

The sun beamed onto the thick snow-covered branches. Ryan could instantly imagine the tree strung with lights and garlands, his family's ornaments hanging from the branches and his grandmother's star beaming from the top. The tree was just the right height to fill the corner of the living room—not too big, not too small.

"Just right?" Cary asked.

"Yeah. You can tell?"

Cary smiled. "I can tell by the way you're looking at it. Come on, let's chop this sucker down."

They took turns with the ax, thwacking

away at the trunk. Cary listened to Ryan's instructions and went about his task with a concentration that Ryan really needed to stop thinking of as adorable. As the tree fell, Cary grinned.

"Timber!" he called out.

They surveyed the tree, and Ryan couldn't stop smiling. Yep, this was the one.

"So…now what? Do those Orcs carry the tree back for us?"

"Usually old Mr. Barnes would help take the tree back and wrap it up, but I don't want to put him out. Think we can manage it on our own? We're pretty far out."

"As Angelo at the gym would say, this is functional training. Maybe I'll start a new fitness trend: hauling trees. Of course in LA they'd have to be palm trees."

"I think you're on to something there. You should tell *US Weekly*."

Cary laughed and picked up the trunk of the tree. "Stars: they're just like us! They haul Christmas trees through the snow."

Ryan grabbed on as well, and they worked in unison to drag the tree back to the farm's entrance. It wasn't easy work, and after a few minutes sweat moistened the back of Ryan's neck. He put the tree down and scooped up a handful of snow into his mouth. Cary followed suit, his brow furrowed as he tentatively placed some snow on his tongue.

"For the record, we should never eat snow if we're lost in the woods." Ryan put another handful into his mouth, where it melted refreshingly.

"Really? Why not?"

"You can get hypothermia. But I think we're safe here on Mr. Barnes's farm. Even if we got lost, someone would come by sooner or later."

"Huh. What else are you not supposed to do with snow?"

"Well, don't ever eat the yellow snow."

"Ha-ha. That much I know." Cary bent down and picked up another handful before packing it into a misshapen ball. "Should you do this?"

Before Ryan could react, the snowball smacked his face, and he sputtered.

"I've always wanted to throw a snowball." Cary grinned and backed up.

"Oh you asked for it, California boy!"

Laughing and shouting, they did battle, dodging behind trees and firing snowballs at each other. For a newbie, Cary had great aim. He launched a missile that Ryan had to dive to evade.

"Just like throwing out a runner at second!" Cary shouted.

"Except you missed! Need some glasses, huh?"

Back and forth they went, the tree forgotten as they dodged and ducked and hurled snowballs. They were both breathing hard by the time Ryan called for a time-out. "Okay, okay. I think it's safe to say you've got the hang of it. With all the cardio you do, I'll never beat you."

"So you're giving up?" Cary grinned.

"On snowballs? Yes." Ryan dusted off his parka and wet jeans. As Cary reached his hand out to shake, Ryan grabbed him and used Cary's momentary surprise to topple him into the snow. "But we have another tradition here. The snow job."

Before Cary could answer, Ryan ripped the red toque from Cary's head and crammed fistfuls of snow into his hair and down the back of his jacket. Cary squirmed and kicked, laughing so hard his breath hitched.

"Okay, okay. I surrender!"

Ryan straddled Cary's hips and pressed Cary's arms above his head in the snow. "You're an honorary Canadian now." His chest heaving as he caught his breath, Ryan smiled down at his friend.

Cary's face was wet and flushed, and a smile played at his parted lips. His tongue darted out, and Ryan couldn't look away. Desire thundered in Ryan's veins, and before he could stop himself, he leaned down and captured Cary's mouth with his own.

Although Cary's lips were cool, beyond them the heat of his mouth drew Ryan in uncontrollably. Their tongues tangled, and the fire in Ryan's veins shot straight to his cock. It felt so good, and he'd wanted it for *so long*. He breathed Cary in as Cary shook off Ryan's grasp on his wrists and grabbed Ryan's head and—

With a gasp, Ryan sat up and staggered to his feet. "I'm sorry! Jesus. I didn't mean to…"

Cary sat up in the snow. His hair was damp and mussed, and he took a shaky breath. "Ryan…"

Ryan raised his hands. "You don't need to say it. This was just…muscle memory." Shame burned in his gut. *How could I be so stupid?*

Cary blinked. "Muscle memory?"

"You know, from the show. From kissing you on set. I didn't mean to do it just now. You know I don't feel that way about you."

"Right." Cary's face was blank as he reached for the toque and put it back on. "Of course. I know."

Cary was probably in shock, and Ryan prayed he hadn't ruined their friendship. "Seriously, you don't have to worry. You're the last guy I'd want to be with."

As Cary got to his feet, he kept his eyes averted. His voice was tight. "I get it. It was just…an accident. Like you said—muscle memory." He brushed the snow off his jeans. "We should get the tree back."

Great. He can't even look at me. "Yeah. I hope…I don't want things to be weird. Especially with you staying here." *He probably wants to catch the first flight back to LA.*

"Do you want me to leave?" Cary's expression was still impassive, and his gaze was fixed somewhere on the horizon. His shoulders hunched.

"No! Of course not. You're my best friend. Can we just forget this happened?"

"Yeah. It's all good, man. Just like another rehearsal." He reached out his fist, and Ryan bumped it. Cary's lips lifted in a ghost of a smile before he picked up the trunk of the fallen tree and began dragging it. He kept his head down.

"It's *MY* TURN to put on the star!" Amy stamped her foot.

"Uh-uh. You did it last year. Moooom, tell her she can't do it!"

Lisa sighed and swallowed a sip of wine. "Ethan, can't you and your sister do it together?"

Maureen spoke up from the kitchen, where she was pressing shortbread dough into a glass dish and singing along to the jazzy Ella Fitzgerald Christmas album they listened to on repeat every year. "It is Christmas, after all. Santa would want you to cooperate with each other."

Grumbling all the way, Ethan and Amy climbed up on the stepladder. Amy wailed, "I can't reach!"

Tony hoisted her up. "Now you're taller than the tree!"

Amy giggled and reached down to straighten the star as her brother placed it atop the tree. "Lights!"

On cue, Ryan plugged in the cord in the outlet by the fireplace, and the whole tree lit up red, green, blue, pink, and yellow, with the bright white star the crowning jewel. "Ta-da!"

Everyone clapped, and Amy squealed as her father swooped her through the air in his arms. When Ryan stood, he caught Cary's gaze, but Cary quickly glanced away. Ryan's stomach churned, and he tried to hide a grimace as his mother passed out glasses of nog. She put her hand on his forehead.

"I've never seen you turn up your nose at my nog before!"

"I'm fine, Mom." Ryan took a gulp of the

sweet, creamy drink. "See?" His mother always spiked nog with amaretto, and the almond liqueur burned pleasantly in Ryan's throat. Maybe a drink was just what he needed to forget what a complete moron he was. He concentrated on Ella's smoky voice jauntily advising on building a snowman in the meadow and calling him Parson Brown.

He was on his second glass when his mother brought in a tray of sausage rolls and settled onto the couch beside him. Cary was in one of the armchairs, and the rest of the family relaxed in various seats or on the thick carpet. The Christmas tree cast colored light over everyone's faces, and Ryan munched happily on a sausage roll.

Maybe everything would be fine. Sure, it had been a little awkward with Cary since…the incident. But Cary seemed okay, eating his sausage roll and talking to Ethan about the latest edition of *Halo*. It would be fine. He and Cary had been friends for a long time now—at least in Hollywood years—and it was just one stupid kiss. Cary had been nice about it, and they'd move past it. Yes, it would be fine.

"The other day I was waiting in Dr. Feinberg's office."

Ryan snapped his wandering mind back to his mother. "Is everything okay?"

"What? Oh yes. I was just getting a wart on my toe burned off."

Amy wrinkled her nose. "Ewwww!"

"Gotta go with Amy on this one, Mom," Lisa added from the other end of the couch.

"My point is that I was reading about that David Baker. You know, from those movies."

Here we go. "Oh right. Yeah, I heard he came out."

Maureen leaned in and stage-whispered, "And he's single!"

"Mom, I don't even know him."

"But you're both actors! Of course you know him. Don't you think he's handsome?"

"Maureen, give the boy a break." Ryan's father glanced up from the fishing magazine he was flipping through.

Ignoring her husband, Maureen turned to Cary. "Do you know him?"

Cary shrugged. "Not really. I met him once at the Golden Globes. He did a movie with my father."

"You see? Ryan, you should get Cary to introduce you. Cary, don't you think they'd make a lovely couple?"

"Yeah. Sure." Cary fiddled with his cocktail napkin, tearing it into neat strips.

"*Mom.* Enough. I know you mean well, but I don't need any help with my love life."

"Well, it *has* been forever since you've had a boyfriend," Lisa muttered.

"*Et tu, Brute?*" Ryan glared. Okay, it was true he hadn't dated anyone seriously in…well, since he met Cary. "I don't have time for a boyfriend. We work fifteen-hour days."

"But you don't work in the summer," Tony said. "And Cary has time for a girlfriend."

Ryan clenched his jaw. "How do you even know that?"

"Maria follows Cary's love life like it's a hockey pool." To Cary, he added, "That must be weird, huh?"

Cary shifted in his seat and shrugged, clearly incredibly uncomfortable. God, it was bad enough Ryan had crossed the line and kissed him—now everyone was going to start asking about Amanda. Ryan jumped in before anyone else could say anything. "Look, when I meet Mr. Right, you'll all be the first to know, okay?"

Jack cleared his throat. "Yes, I think that's enough grilling for now. It's Christmas, not the Inquisition."

Ryan's mother sighed. "I'm sorry, dear. I just want you to be happy. Isn't there anyone you're interested in?"

The memory of the dimples in Cary's cheeks and the warm taste of his mouth invaded Ryan's mind. "No! There isn't." He kept his gaze locked on his glass.

"Mom, I think we should go check on the roast. Kids, set the table, please." Lisa gave Ryan's shoulder a quick squeeze as she passed by behind the couch.

When Ryan dared to look over, Cary was reading one of Jack's fishing magazines. He was apparently engrossed, and didn't look up once until they were called to dinner.

TUGGING AT THE COLLAR of his ridiculous reindeer pajamas, Ryan tried to get comfortable in his narrow bed. He heard Cary climbing the ladder and debated whether to fake sleep. But Cary appeared before he could decide, and their eyes met. Ryan swore a current of electricity sparked in the air between them, but clearly he'd had too much eggnog.

Cary's hair was damp, and he gave his face another swipe with his towel before hanging it over the end of his bed. His T-shirt clung to his lean muscles, and Ryan thought about what Cary had said the night before about sleeping nude.

Stop. Danger. Retreat!

Ryan stared up at the neon solar system as Cary flicked the light off and climbed into bed across the narrow room. Ryan knew he should say something and was batting around ideas when Cary beat him to it.

"Hey, do you think your parents would mind if I call long distance tomorrow? I'll pay for it. I'd use my cell, but no service, so…"

"Sure. It's no problem. And you can give your folks our number in case they want to call. My parents won't mind at all."

There was a beat of silence. "Why would they call?"

"Oh. Tomorrow's Christmas Eve. I thought…but right, your family's not into Christmas." Ryan's palms itched, and he felt like an idiot. It was like every word out of his mouth made everything worse.

"No. Anyway, I'm going to call Amanda and apologize."

Ryan bolted up in bed and came extremely close to whacking his head on the slanted ceiling. "*Amanda?* But I thought…I mean, you said she wasn't right for you."

"I overreacted. I should apologize and try to work it out with her. I can probably move up my flight and get home for New Year's. It's her favorite holiday."

"Right. Sure. Yeah, you can use the phone whenever you want."

"Cool. Thanks."

As the minutes ticked by, Ryan stared up at the glowing planets and stars. He listened for Cary to fall asleep, but in the tense silence, he didn't seem to be sleeping either. Ryan cursed himself again. For a year and a half he'd kept his feelings in check, and in one careless moment of want he threw it all away.

Ryan couldn't blame him for being upset. Cary trusted him to be a good friend—not to put the moves on him. Especially when Cary was fresh off a breakup. Not to mention *straight*. He came for the holidays to relax and get away from it all, and Ryan had just made everything worse. He couldn't blame Cary at all for wanting to leave.

As the minutes ticked by, Ryan found himself wishing he could ask Santa for a do-over.

Chapter Four

"SEE HOW THICK that ice is? Tell your mother she's worrying for nothing."

Ryan nodded dutifully. "Yes, Dad. Although this is early to have the hut out. I can't remember the last time you fished in December. It's nice."

Next to him, Cary shifted on the wooden bench, his knee brushing Ryan's. Quarters were tight in the hut with Ryan, Cary, and Tony squeezed onto the bench. On the other side of the fishing hole sawed into the ice, Ryan's father sat back on his folding chair.

A fire in a metal drum kept the hut relatively warm, and of course the wooden walls and roof protected them from the wind. A chimney funneled the smoke from the fire outside and a gas lantern hung from a hook in the ceiling.

"Now I know it isn't much, Cary, but I've

caught thousands of fish in this hut. Plenty of people today want all the mod cons, but all I need is a seat, a fire, and a hole in the ice for my pole."

Cary smiled. "It's great. I wish I'd been able to go fishing as a kid." He ran his gloved fingers over the rod and reel he held. "I love it out here."

"You're not too cold? It's a far cry from Malibu, I know." Jack smiled kindly.

Cary's lips were practically blue, but he shook his head. "I'm good. How many years have you had this place?"

"Hmm. I suppose it's almost twenty years now. Ryan was about five when we bought it. It was awfully run-down, but we fixed it up over the years. If Ryan had his way, he'd have built us a mansion, but it suits us just fine the way it is."

Ryan rolled his eyes. "I didn't want to build a mansion. I just wanted to help pay for the work on the roof. You know you can't put it off for another winter."

"And I won't. I'm retiring this summer, and I'll have plenty of time to do the work."

"Ryan said you work for the government. Are you looking forward to retirement?" Cary asked.

Jack grinned. "Am I ever. I've spent long enough as a civil servant. Have to spend some time catching fish before the bay dries up. Water levels keep going down and last year we barely had a white Christmas."

Ryan and Tony shared a glance. Jack could talk for hours about global warming and the water levels and the impact on the environment—and fishing.

Tony stood. "Well, I've had enough for today, fellas. I'll take the catch in."

Jack checked his watch and sighed. "I suppose we should call it a day."

"I just want to catch one more. Is it okay if I stay?" Cary asked.

"Sure. I'll stay with you," Ryan quickly replied.

His father chuckled as he stood and stretched his arms over his head. His hands brushed the ceiling. "I've never seen you so eager to fish, son. I used to have to drag you out here."

Shrugging, Ryan fiddled with his rod. "It's not so bad after all."

"I suppose you're older and wiser and can finally appreciate the finer things in life." Jack ruffled Ryan's hair, and Ryan ducked away with a laugh.

Ryan and Cary stood so Tony could squeeze by. Ryan's rod dipped with an insistent tug, and he quickly sat back down to reel in the fish while Cary lifted the bucket.

"You two okay to take out the lures? Just remember what I showed you," Jack said. "We'll take the cooler, and you can bring the rest in the bucket. Don't be too long. Your mother will have dinner on the table soon."

"Thanks, Mr. Drake. We won't be long."

"It's Jack, remember?"

Cary smiled. "Thanks, Jack." He stood as Jack and Tony left. When he sat back down, he left room between him and Ryan on the bench. "You don't have to stay if you don't want to."

Ryan shifted and let out the line on his rod a bit. "Do you want to be alone? I can go."

"Whatever. If you wanna stay, it's cool."

"Okay." Ryan hated the awkwardness between them. He and Cary had always been so comfortable with each other, and now Ryan had changed everything. He cleared his throat. "I have to say I didn't peg you for an ice fishing fan."

Cary bobbed his rod up and down and shrugged. "It's peaceful."

They sat in silence for a few minutes until the words that had been swirling through Ryan's mind spewed out of his mouth. "I don't think you should call Amanda."

Cary visibly tensed. "Why not?"

"You said it yourself. You two aren't right for each other."

"Yeah, well. Maybe I don't know what's right for me. I thought I did, but I was totally wrong."

Ryan frowned. "What do you mean?"

"Forget it." Cary kept his gaze on the hole in the ice where their fishing lines disappeared. He sighed. "Maybe I should just go. This is your Christmas with your family, and I just barged in."

"It's your Christmas too." The thought of Cary leaving was unbearable. "Besides, it's Christmas Eve. You wouldn't even be able to get a flight out."

"It's just…" Cary rubbed a hand over his face.

"What?" Ryan's throat scratched. He realized his hands were shaking, and not from the cold. He clamped his rod into one of the metal holders his dad had fashioned and gulped from a thermos of now stale coffee.

"Being here with you…it's hard."

Ryan's eyes burned, and he blinked rapidly, looking everywhere but at Cary. "I understand. I don't want you to be uncomfortable. If you want to leave, I guess that would be best."

"Sure. Okay. I'm sure Amanda will take me back. I could meet her at the spa. I'll get a flight somehow." Cary's voice was strained wire thin.

He had to say it. "I just think you deserve

better."

"Why do you care?" Cary asked sharply.

Ryan blinked. "You're my friend. When I moved to LA, I lost touch with most of my friends from Toronto, and it's hard to meet anyone there who's real, you know?" He was babbling, but he couldn't stop. "I'd go to parties and bars, but it wasn't until I met you and started working on the show that I stopped feeling totally alone. You're not just my friend—you're my best friend."

Cary jumped to his feet and began reeling in his line. "Right. You've made it very clear, Ryan."

"What?" Nausea roiled in Ryan's gut, and he stood beside Cary. This was all going wrong. *Please don't hate me.* "If this is about yesterday—"

"Look, I get it." Cary finished reeling in his line and stared at the lure swaying back and forth. "I'm an idiot, okay? I thought... God, I denied how I felt for so long, but I actually thought there was something between us."

Ryan felt as though all the air had been sucked out of the hut. He gaped as his brain struggled to process. "You...us?"

Cary winced. "I'm sorry. Stupid, huh? I always thought we had a connection as friends, but..."

"But?" Ryan could barely get the word out.

"But once Steven and Kishi got together on the show and I got to kiss you…" He blew out a long breath, a miserable expression darkening his face as he closed his eyes. "I realized how much I want you. I thought you wanted me too, but you were just doing your job."

Cary opened his eyes again but kept his gaze averted. "You made it really clear yesterday that you're not interested. I imagined it, and now I've made things all weird and embarrassing. So I'll just leave, and we can go back to normal in LA and try to forget this ever happened. Okay?"

"You…feel…" Ryan's head spun violently. "For me?" Disbelief and hope and affection melded in his chest, and Ryan couldn't stop the incredulous laughter that bubbled up. "You *like* me?"

Cary leaned his rod against the wall and crossed his arms. The tips of his ears burned red. "I'm sorry. It's ridiculous, and you don't like me back and—"

"Oh my God, shut up and kiss me," Ryan blurted as he yanked Cary against him and pressed their lips together.

His hands tangled in Cary's hair, and Cary's mouth opened and their tongues met. Cary gripped Ryan's hips, and they tumbled against the wall of the hut, fortunately missing the fishing hole as the bench tipped over. The lantern swung wildly overhead, casting light and shadow over them.

Gasping in a breath, Ryan pulled back. "I must be dreaming."

"You said you didn't want me." Cary stared, face so open and vulnerable, his lip caught between his teeth.

Ryan could only laugh. "I thought you'd be *mad* at me. I thought you were straight."

"I don't know what I am. All I know is that I want you." He wedged his thigh between Ryan's.

Cary kissed him again, his tongue sweeping into Ryan's mouth as they rubbed against each other. They were wearing too many layers, and their hands were clumsy as they grabbed and stroked, desperate to touch, but not willing to stop kissing.

Ryan thought he might come from the taste of Cary's mouth alone, or from the breathy little moans that escaped Cary's lips when Ryan managed to get his hands on Cary's denim-clad ass under his parka. They ground together, both hard in their jeans.

As they rutted, they exhaled in stolen whispers between kisses.

"I've wanted this for so long. Want you so much," Ryan murmured. "I thought you'd hate me if you knew. Thought I'd ruin everything."

"I could never hate you." Cary kissed him again, his tongue sliding over Ryan's. "I was going crazy. Wanted you so bad. I jerked off in my trailer every day before our scenes so I wouldn't get hard when I touched you."

Moaning, Ryan gripped Cary's ass tighter and hooked a leg over his hip to get a better angle. *If this is a dream, I don't ever want to wake up.* His leaking dick was trapped in his jeans, and he was going to come in his pants like a kid, but he didn't care. "I never thought…" They rocked together, and Ryan's balls tingled. He brushed Cary's cheeks with his fingertips. "I can't believe you want me too."

They kissed again, and after a few more frantic thrusts, Ryan came, his legs trembling as the pleasure crashed over him. Cary sucked on Ryan's neck, his hips still seeking friction. Ryan sank to his knees and pushed Cary against the wall, a new desperation whipping through him like electricity through a wire.

He managed to unzip Cary's jeans. The parka was awkward and heavy and in the way, but Ryan just pushed it up as he tugged Cary's jeans open and pulled out his cock. It was heavy and red, the tip glistening. Ryan sucked it into his mouth and swirled his tongue around the shaft, savoring the musky taste and scent. He could do this all day.

Cary was practically whimpering, his fingers tight in Ryan's hair as Ryan worked him with his mouth. *I'm sucking Cary's cock. This is actually happening.*

"Ry, I'm gonna—" Cary's hips stuttered, and he cried out.

Ryan swallowed convulsively and milked every last drop of Cary's orgasm. Sagging against the wall of the hut, Cary caressed Ryan's hair and breathed heavily. There was a sheen of sweat above his lip, and Ryan got to his feet and kissed him soundly.

Cary pressed their foreheads together. "Feels so good with you." He took a deep breath. "So I guess I wasn't imagining it? You do want me?"

Ryan took Cary's face in his hands. "From the day we met." He ran his thumb over Cary's bottom lip. "Wanted to kiss you. Wanted…everything." He leaned in and—

"Boys!" Maureen's voice echoed distantly on the wind.

With another kiss, they reluctantly separated and straightened their jackets. Fortunately their parkas and layers would cover up the wet spots on their jeans and they could change before dinner. Ryan extinguished the fire and lantern and pushed open the door of the hut. The last flare of orange light from the setting sun splashed over Georgian Bay, reflecting softly on the snow.

"Wow." Cary joined him outside. He looked up. "Maybe we can look at the stars tonight. Can you see them from your room?"

Ryan's body thrummed with desire. He swallowed hard. "Yeah."

Cary met his gaze, the hunger in his own eyes clear. "I'm pretty tired from fishing. Think I'll have an early night."

Ryan nodded. "Me too."

"Are you coming?" Maureen called out, echoing across the frozen bay from the deck of the cottage about a hundred yards away.

Glancing at each other, Ryan and Cary actually giggled. Ryan called back. "Yes!"

They started back across the ice, slip-sliding in some places where the snow had been blown thin, laughter echoing in the stillness of the winter night.

IN THE END THEY had to sit through not only dinner, but Scrabble *and* Monopoly. As eager as Ryan was to be alone with Cary again, he was afraid everyone would know exactly what was on their minds if they tried to get away early. As it was he felt like everyone knew, even though no one was acting any differently.

"Go straight to jail and do not collect two hundred dollars," Ethan recited. With a groan, he moved his top hat to the jail spot. "This freaking blows."

As Lisa and Tony scolded Ethan for his language, Ryan glanced at Cary across the dining table and found Cary watching him. Cary quickly lowered his gaze to fiddle with his colored money. Ryan still couldn't believe this was actually happening. He'd been so horrified when he kissed Cary at the tree farm, but Cary had *wanted* it.

It didn't seem possible. Ryan had worked so hard to hide his own feelings that he'd somehow missed spotting Cary's. He had so many questions. Was Cary gay? When did he start feeling this way? Were they going to be a couple now?

"Uncle Ryan?"

Ryan focused on Amy, who sat at the head of the table. "Uh-huh?"

"Why are you so happy? You don't have any good properties. Not even a railroad."

"I know. But it's Christmas. Of course I'm happy." He kept his gaze away from Cary. "I'm here with my favorite niece, after all."

Amy frowned. "I'm your only niece."

"What? Are you sure? Lisa, you don't have any other daughters hanging around? I swear there were a couple more."

Lisa pretended to ponder it. "Hon, what did we do with those other daughters?"

Tony stroked his chin. "Now that you mention it, I think we might have left them in Florida when we went to visit my folks in St. Pete's that winter."

"No you didn't!" Amy giggled. "I'm your only daughter."

Jack spoke up from where he lounged in his recliner by the fireplace beside the Christmas tree. "I do seem to recall some other little girls. I thought they'd been eaten by bears."

"No!" Amy shrieked, laughing and shaking her head.

Ryan's mom brought out a plate of shortbread from the kitchen and a tray of tea and hot chocolate. As everyone laughed and teased Amy, Ryan passed Cary his mug. Their fingers brushed together, and beneath the table, Cary pressed his foot against Ryan's. Even through their woolen socks, Ryan swore he could feel a spark.

Finally it was time for bed. The stockings had been hung from the mantel above the fireplace for days, but Amy still insisted on making sure they were all there—along with a plate of shortbread and a glass of milk. She peered at Cary, brow furrowed, and then back at the fireplace.

"Are you sure Santa will know you're here, Uncle Cary?" she asked. "He might get confused. We should put your name on your stocking."

Cary smiled. "It's okay, sweetheart. I don't have a stocking here. I'm sure Santa will leave me my presents at home in LA."

"Of course you have a stocking!" Amy seemed scandalized at the very thought that he wouldn't. "See?" She pointed to each stocking. "Gran, Granddad, Mommy, Daddy, Uncle Ryan, Ethan, and you. But yours doesn't have your name on it."

For a moment, Cary didn't say anything. He cleared his throat. "That's okay. I'm sure Santa will know." He turned to Ryan's parents. "Thank you. You didn't need to do that."

Maureen waved her hand. "Nonsense. Everyone needs a stocking at Christmas! I would have sewn your name on it, but I've been up to my elbows in turkey and breadcrumbs, and my darling daughter can't sew on a button to save her life."

"Because she works twelve-hour shifts at the hospital and chooses to pay people to sew for her," Lisa replied.

Maureen scoffed good-naturedly. "She says that as if I wasn't a nurse myself for thirty-five years."

"But you're superwoman, remember?" Lisa laughed and gave her mother a kiss. "All right, kids. Off to brush your teeth and go to bed, or you'll be on the naughty list."

As Amy gasped and headed for the stairs, Ethan rolled his eyes. "It's not like Santa's even re—"

"Really paying attention tonight since he's too busy?" Tony asked with a stern look. "Santa's a man of many talents. Now get going." Under his breath he added, "And don't ruin it for your sister."

"All right, all right. Sorry." Ethan followed Amy upstairs, with Lisa and Tony on his heels.

Jack stretched his arms over his head and yawned. "That's me as well. Ryan, do you and Cary want to do the honors?" He nodded to the plate of shortbread.

"Either that or I put them back in the tin. I'm stuffed," Maureen added.

"Sure. Cary and I can polish them off." Ryan kissed her cheek. "Thanks, Mom. Merry Christmas."

"Merry Christmas. Sleep tight."

As his parents got settled upstairs, Ryan turned off the rest of the lamps until only the Christmas tree was lit by the fireplace. Cary stood by a window nearby, the colored lights catching in his blond hair.

"It's snowing again."

Ryan joined him at the window and, with a quick glance at the stairs, wrapped his arms around Cary from behind. Although Cary was broader, Ryan felt as if their bodies fit together perfectly. He kissed the back of Cary's neck. "I feel like every Christmas wish I ever made just came true."

Cary put his hand over Ryan's and threaded their fingers together. "I never made any Christmas wishes, but I guess I got on the nice list this year."

They watched the snow drifting down outside, the Christmas tree behind them reflecting softly in the glass.

"I guess we have a lot to talk about," Cary whispered.

Ryan pressed kisses along Cary's neck, finding a place behind his ear that made Cary's breath hitch. "I guess so."

Cary turned in Ryan's arms. "But I don't wanna talk."

Ryan wasn't sure how long they stood there kissing. They explored each other's mouths slowly and deeply, and he was light-headed by the time he took Cary's hand and led him upstairs. Somehow they made it up the ladder to the third floor while still kissing, even if they ended up in a heap on the bedroom floor at the top.

They quickly pulled their clothes off and tossed their sweaters and jeans aside. The carpet was rather worn, so Ryan pulled down his duvet and spread it out before leaning back. Cary straddled his hips, and Ryan drank in the sight of Cary's bare skin in the cool moonlight. He ran his hands over Cary's chest and muscular shoulders, exploring every inch.

"You look like you've never seen me shirtless before," Cary blurted with a nervous laugh.

"Not like this." Ryan propped himself up on an elbow and slowly sucked one of Cary's nipples. "Not when I can *really* look." He sucked on the other nipple and drew his fingertips down Cary's spine before teasing the crack of his ass. He whispered against Cary's skin. "Not when I can really touch."

With a groan, Cary tangled his hand in Ryan's hair and crushed their mouths together. He lengthened out on top of Ryan and thrust against him desperately. "Want you so much, Ry."

The feel of Cary's lean, powerful body against his own from head to toes was intoxicating. Ryan spread his legs and urged him closer. Their cocks rubbed together, and Ryan trembled with a feverish want and *need*. Any minute now he'd wake up and this would all be a dream, but until then he clung to Cary.

"I don't...I don't know what I'm doing," Cary muttered. "I mean...I've never...with a guy. Not really."

"It's okay." Ryan forced himself to take a long, deep breath and stilled his hips, even though his throbbing dick protested vigorously. "We can go slow." What he really wanted was Cary's cock in his ass immediately, but he didn't want to scare him off.

Cary shifted a little of his weight onto his hip and reached down to wrap his hand around Ryan's shaft. He stroked tentatively.

Biting back a groan, Ryan thrust into the heat of his palm. "This works."

"You said once..." Cary took a deep breath. "Remember the wrap party for season one when we all got wasted and played truth or dare?"

"Vaguely?" It was difficult to concentrate on anything but Cary's hand on his cock. Ryan desperately tried to remember what he said in the haze of Corona and tequila shots but came up blank.

"You said you were a bottom." Cary took a deep breath and rushed on. "SoifyoulikeitthenmaybecanIfuckyou?"

Ryan laughed and took Cary's face in his hands. He kissed him hard. "I've wanted your cock inside me every day since our screen test."

Cary's cheeks dimpled. "So that's a yes?" He teased the slit of Ryan's dick with his thumb.

"Yes, yes, y—shit."

Cary froze. "What? Did I…?"

"I don't have anything with me." He cursed himself. "And I don't think Santa will leave condoms and lube in our stockings tonight."

"Oh." Cary relaxed and kissed Ryan. "It's okay. I brought some. Just in case."

Ryan's whole body tingled. *Just in case he could have sex with me.* "You must have been a Boy Scout."

Cary's smile was rueful. "Nope. I tried one year, but I missed half the meetings because I had to go on location with my dad."

"Well, you're going to earn a badge tonight. Probably a few different ones."

Chuckling, Cary hurried over to his suitcase. Ryan shivered without the heat of Cary's body, but soon enough Cary was back with a box of condoms and a tube of lube that looked like it came from Costco.

"You *definitely* came prepared."

On his knees by Ryan's feet, Cary flicked the cap with a grin and squeezed some lube onto his fingers. Then he paused, brow furrowed. "They never really do this part in the videos."

"So you've been watching gay porn?" The

thought made Ryan's throat go dry.

"Uh-huh. I was curious."

How is this real life? "Did you like it?"

Cary nodded, his Adam's apple bobbing as he swallowed thickly.

His low voice sounding foreign to his own ears, Ryan asked, "Did you jerk off while you watched?"

Another nod.

Did you think about me? Ryan couldn't quite get his next question out. His throat was too dry.

"I imagined it was you," Cary whispered. "That I was fucking you."

Ryan spread his legs wide and brought his knees up, exposing his hole. He reached for Cary's hand. "Use your fingers. Open me up for your cock."

His breathing shallow, Cary nudged his slick fingertip into Ryan's ass, just barely. Ryan reached for Cary's wrist impatiently. "More. It's okay."

"It feels good?" Cary's gaze was locked on Ryan's hole as he worked him open with one long finger and then two. "God, you're so tight." He shuddered and jerked his straining cock a few times.

Ryan jerked his head in a nod, pressing his lips together to swallow his moans as Cary pushed into him. He spread his legs even farther, totally unselfconscious in a way he'd never been with anyone else before. "I do this to myself and pretend it's you," he confessed.

With a groan, Cary leaned over and kissed him. He wiggled a third finger inside Ryan. "Is it enough?"

Groaning at the delicious fullness, he nodded. "You now."

When Cary pulled his fingers out, Ryan couldn't help but squeeze at them with his ass, not wanting to let them go. Sitting back on his heels, Cary rolled on a condom and coated himself with another squirt of lube. His cock glistened in the moonlight, and his body looked like a marble statue. *So beautiful.*

Ryan's legs were already pulled up, but he spread them even more and lifted his ass as Cary lined himself up. Lips parted, Cary swallowed thickly.

"God, you're amazing. I wanna fuck you so hard."

Ryan's heart thumped so loudly he was sure it would wake his family. "Do it." He gripped Cary's waist and urged him closer, not able to bite back the moan as Cary finally inched inside him. Their eyes locked, and Ryan bore down, reveling in the burning stretch in his ass as Cary filled him.

"Ryan. God, this is…" Cary groaned as he filled Ryan to the hilt. His arms shook slightly where he held his weight. "Better than any-thing."

"It's okay. Let go."

Ryan wrapped his arms around Cary's shoulders and opened his mouth in a silent cry as Cary plunged in and out of him. Even though the attic room got chilly in the night, they were both sweating as they rocked together, kissing with open mouths and gasping softly.

Cary's inside me.

He could hardly believe it was happening. Cary was fucking him, his thrusts getting more and more chaotic as they got closer to the edge. He hoisted one of Ryan's legs over his shoulder and went even deeper, brushing against Ryan's prostate.

"There. *There*," Ryan cried out, before slap-ping a hand over his own mouth. There was no door on the attic room, but at least the closest bedroom to the ladder was the kids', and they would sleep through an earthquake.

"You feel so good," Cary whispered, eyes wide. "Wanted to fuck you for so long. Wanna come inside you and fill you up. See my cum dripping out of your ass…"

Ryan's balls tightened. "Fuck, yes." He im-agined they didn't have to use a condom—that

Cary could shoot deep inside him. "Harder."

His thighs flexing, Cary tried to hit the right spot again. When he did, Ryan could only close his eyes and ride it out. He snaked a hand between them and jacked his leaking cock, so close to the edge already.

"You're the best I've ever had. Knew you would be." Panting, Cary pushed even deeper. "So good."

Lips parted, Ryan teetered on the edge before another thrust from Cary sent him over. He splashed his chest, coming in long spurts that had his whole body trembling. He clamped down, and Cary threw his head back as he drove into Ryan's ass until he shook with release. Eyes closed and mouth open, his face was a mask of sheer bliss before he collapsed on top of Ryan.

Chests heaving, they lay in a heap until Cary rolled away and tossed the tied condom into the garbage can by Ryan's dresser. He rolled back and peered at Ryan with a frown. Tentatively, he reached down and skimmed his fingertips over Ryan's stretched hole.

"Was it…I didn't hurt you, did I?"

Shaking his head, Ryan drew Cary down for a gentle kiss. "It was perfect."

Cary's smile lit up his face. "It kind of was. You're…" He caressed Ryan's hair, brushing it back from his forehead. "You're amazing. The best Christmas present ever."

Ryan laughed softly. "You too." He grabbed his discarded briefs and wiped off his chest. "Hey, you want to look at the stars?"

Cary squinted at the window. "I think it's snowing too much to see them."

With a smile, Ryan got up and led Cary to his bed, bringing the duvet with them. It was a tight squeeze in the narrow bed, but they found a comfortable position with their legs tangled and heads together on the pillow. Cary laughed quietly as he noticed the glowing stickers stuck to the slanted ceiling.

"Thanks for showing me the stars," he whispered.

It was almost four o'clock when Ryan woke with a start and tried to inch out of bed. Cary blinked blearily, his arms tightening around Ryan. "Where are you going?"

"Santa needs to eat his cookies or I'm in big trouble in the morning."

"I'll come with you."

They pulled on their pajamas and tiptoed downstairs where the gentle glow of the Christmas tree waited. They ate the cookies and shared the glass of now warm milk, trying to see who could make the biggest milk moustache before kissing them away and creeping back to bed for a long winter's nap.

Chapter Five

"UNCLE RYAN! UNCLE CARY! It's Christmas!"

Ryan opened his eyes to find Amy at the side of his bed in the dark, her cheeks flushed and a reindeer antler headband holding back her curls. He was spooning Cary—and had been drooling on the back of his neck—and was very relieved they'd put on their pajamas. He felt Cary tense in his arms. Ryan cleared his throat and held Cary close. "Merry Christmas, Amy. What time is it?"

"Six thirty. Mom said if I woke her before seven the Ghost of Christmas Past would haunt me tonight. But you guys can come down and open your stockings! We're allowed. We got Silly Putty, and Ethan already lost his in the woodpile. Come and see all the presents Santa brought!"

"We'll be right down. Go help Ethan find his Silly Putty."

"Okay!" With boundless energy, Amy raced to the ladder and practically jumped down to the second floor.

Cary sprung out of bed and paced. "I'm sorry. I should have gone back to my bed. Do you think…will she say anything?"

Ryan waved his hand. "The only thing on her mind is what Santa left her under the tree."

Running his fingers through his disheveled hair, Cary exhaled. His pajama bottoms were low on his hips and his T-shirt rode up over his hard stomach. "Okay. It's not that I don't…you didn't seem to want to tell your family. Right?"

It was a great question, and Ryan wasn't sure how he felt. It was all so new, and he could hardly believe in the slowly dawning morning light that it hadn't all been a fevered dream. "Yeah, I guess we have stuff to talk about first. Are you…how are you feeling?"

Cary's lips twitched into a tentative smile. "Good." He reached for Ryan's hand and tugged him lightly out of bed and into a sweet kiss. He smoothed his palm over Ryan's ass. "Reindeer pajamas have never been so sexy."

There was a crash from downstairs, and Ryan reluctantly broke away from Cary. "I'd better get down there before they break something else. My mom's probably in the shower. She usually gets up around six to put all the presents under the tree and fill the stockings. Sorry, there's always a line for the bathroom."

"It's okay. It's nice, everyone being here together and not spread out over a dozen rooms. I like it." Cary traced Ryan's cheekbone with his knuckle and then leaned in and slowly licked a spot on Ryan's jaw near his ear. "I've wanted to lick that mole for so long," he murmured.

With a groan, Ryan stepped away. "Okay, we've got to get downstairs or I'm going to throw you down and have my way with you."

Cary's eyes twinkled. "That was definitely on my Christmas list."

"WHAT'S THIS?" CARY took his place at the dinner table and prodded the brightly wrapped cylinder by his plate.

Amy frowned. "It's a Christmas cracker."

Cary picked it up and peered into one open end. The cardboard tube was wrapped in shiny gold-and-red paper with both ends tied off near the middle. "What's it for?"

"For fun, I suppose," Maureen answered with a wink as she brought in the cranberry sauce and added it to the incredible spread of sliced turkey, stuffing, yams, beans, and crispy roasted potatoes on the table. "Considering how fond Americans are of fireworks, I'm surprised this tradition was lost."

"Here." Ryan picked up his own cracker by one end and held out the other to Cary beside him. "Put your thumb on the little stick inside. Now give Ethan the other end of yours. When we're all ready, then we pull at the same time."

Once they all had one end of a cracker in their hands, they counted in unison. "One, two, three!"

Loud *pops* filled the air as the crackers tore apart and the contents went flying. Ryan fished his toy out of the gravy with his spoon, slurping the tiny pinball game into his mouth to clean it off, much to the delight of Amy and Ethan.

Cary peered into his torn cracker with a grin and shook out the contents—a toy, a joke, and a purple tissue-paper crown. He unfolded it and put it on. "This is awesome."

Somehow Cary still looked incredibly hand-some wearing a ridiculous paper hat. Ryan put on his red one. "Just wait until you hear the jokes."

"Why did the cow cross the road?" Tony asked, reading from a curled piece of paper. He waited a beat. "To get to the udder side."

They all groaned, and once they had on

their hats, Jack retrieved the camera from the living room and stood at the end of the table. "Everyone say Merry Christmas!"

"Merry Christmas!"

Twenty minutes later, Cary rubbed his belly and shook his head. "My trainer's going to kill me, but that was the best turkey I've ever had. How do you get the stuffing so perfect?"

Maureen sipped her glass of Pinot Noir at the head of the table near the kitchen, her yellow crown askew. "Years of experience. And thank you." She reached for the platter in the center of the table. "You're sure you don't want more?"

Cary raised his hand. "Thank you, but I couldn't."

"There's still dessert though, right?" Ethan asked. He spun the top that had come with his Christmas cracker.

"It wouldn't be Christmas without plum pudding and mincemeat pies," Jack said. He folded his orange hat beside his plate. "But I think we all need a breather first."

There were nods and murmurs of assent, and Ryan got up to help clear the table. Cary leaped up beside him and began piling plates. "Thank you again for an incredible dinner, Maureen."

She fingered the new pearl necklace she wore. "My pleasure, dear. Thank you for the wonderful gifts. They really are too much."

"It was the least I could do after you welcomed me into your home." Cary picked up a stack of plates and carried them to the kitchen.

"Don't be silly. Any *friend* of Ryan's is part of the family," Lisa said as she reached for more wine.

Tony deftly maneuvered the bottle out of her reach. "Come on, let's put on some coffee."

Ryan gave him a grateful smile as Lisa grumbled but followed Tony to the kitchen.

Once they finished coffee and dessert, they all flopped in the living room, too stuffed to do anything but watch one of the new movies Santa had put under the tree. Christmas dinner was always early, and by nine they were all in bed.

Well, his family was in bed. Ryan was pacing by his, waiting for Cary to finish in the bathroom. All day he'd had to keep his hands in his pockets to stop himself from reaching out to touch. It didn't seem real that he *could* touch Cary now.

"I like the new PJs." Cary stepped off the top of the ladder.

Ryan flushed. He'd stripped down to his white briefs while he waited. "Thanks."

"Guess I'm overdressed." Cary pulled his T-shirt over his head and kicked off his pajama bottoms. He wasn't wearing underwear. He switched off the light, but the moon was still bright.

Ryan's throat went dry as Cary stalked toward him. "That's a good look for you."

As he sank to his knees, Cary reached for Ryan's hips. He nuzzled Ryan through his briefs, taking deep breaths, his exhalations sending goose bumps over Ryan's thighs. Cary tugged down Ryan's briefs, and Ryan stepped out of them. His pulse zoomed, blood rushing in his ears as Cary closed his lips over the head of his dick.

His initial tentativeness, with little kisses and experimental swipes of his tongue, soon evaporated, and Cary sucked Ryan deeply. He bobbed his head back and forth, his lips stretched around Ryan's throbbing cock. As the blissful minutes passed, Ryan reached up to hold on to the slant of the ceiling, his legs shaking as he watched his fantasies come to life—Cary on his knees for him, saliva dribbling down his chin, his mouth so hot and tight and—

Ryan tugged on Cary's head to warn him as his balls tightened, but Cary just sucked harder, his cheeks hollowing. Ryan saw bursts of color as he pulsed into Cary's mouth, biting his tongue to stop his cries. He stroked Cary's hair. "Jesus. You're a natural."

Cary tensed and got to his feet. He swiped

his hand over his mouth and wouldn't meet Ryan's gaze. "Thanks," he muttered.

Blinking, Ryan reached for him and cupped his cheek. "What just happened? Where did you go?"

Eyes still averted, Cary shrugged. "I don't know. Sorry."

"Come on." Ryan took his hand and urged him onto his back on Ryan's bed. He straddled his thighs and stroked Cary's chest, teasing his nipples and the light hair sprinkled there. "You're beautiful."

Cary opened his mouth as if to argue, but Ryan cut him off by swallowing his cock. Cary was already hard and leaking, and Ryan traced the vein on the underside of his shaft with his tongue as he reached down and caressed Cary's balls and the sensitive skin behind them. He wanted to lift Cary's ass and bury his face there with his tongue inside, but Cary was already whimpering softly.

Lips stretched wide, Ryan watched as Cary came, his long eyelashes dark on his cheeks, ecstasy written on his slack face. Ryan swallowed as much as he could and licked up the semen that dripped out of his mouth. Cary had been gripping Ryan's shoulders, and now his hands fell away.

"God. I've never…it's so good with you."

Ryan stretched out and pulled the duvet over them. He rested his head on Cary's chest and listened to his heartbeat slow back to normal. "It's the best it's ever been." He skimmed his fingers over Cary's stomach and circled his belly button. "Better than I dreamed."

They were quiet, and after a while the rhythm of Cary's breathing began to lull Ryan to sleep. But then Cary spoke, just a whisper.

"Do you really think I'm a natural?"

Ryan opened his eyes, but kept his head resting where it was. "I do. Is that…okay?"

"When I was thirteen, my dad did that terrible movie—the one with the aliens that farted poisonous gas? Anyway, I had to spend the whole summer in New Mexico. It was so hot you could barely move."

"Uh-huh?" Ryan wasn't sure where Cary was going with this, but he waited quietly.

"The director's son was there too, so we hung out. His name was Matt. We played video games and stuff. He was fifteen. He had an indoor pool at their rental house, and we'd spend hours in there goofing around. One day he dared me to go skinny dipping. So we did, and we were roughhousing and…I'm sure you see where this is going."

Ryan pressed a kiss to Cary's chest. "Yeah.

Go on."

"We jerked each other off, and it felt so good. The furthest I'd been with a girl was second base, and this was like…heaven. We did it every day, just hand jobs. But I really wanted to kiss him, and one afternoon in the pool, I did." Cary went silent.

"What happened?"

"He punched me. Called me a fag. Said if I told anyone what we'd done together he'd tell everyone I was queer and get my father fired. I spent the rest of the summer by myself. I felt guilty every time I jerked off because I couldn't stop thinking about kissing Matt, or some other guy. It had only been for a second when I kissed him, but it wasn't like kissing girls. It turned me on in a different way."

Cary still sounded so ashamed, and it twisted Ryan's heart. He caressed Cary's stomach. "There's nothing wrong with that."

"I…I know. But I don't think my father would agree. I may be named after Cary Grant—and the irony is not lost on me considering the rumors about him—but my dad and grandfather are old-school Republicans. They'd freak if they knew about me. That I'm…whatever I am."

"Gay? You can say it. It won't bite."

"Maybe."

"But you can't say it out loud yet." Ryan wished it didn't make his chest ache hollowly. He wanted to sit up and see Cary's face but part of him was afraid to look.

"The thing is that I don't know if that's the right word. After Matt, I never went near another guy. I told myself it was a phase—just part of growing up. And I really thought it was. Or at least I convinced myself for a while. I've slept with a lot of women, and I liked it. I wasn't faking. I love tits and pussy."

"Okay." Ryan grimaced. "I can't relate, but there's nothing wrong with that. And you also like cock. Clearly."

Cary ran his hand down Ryan's back and over his butt. "And ass. And strong, hairy, male bodies. Cock is…fuck, it's amazing. So what does that make me? Bi?"

"I guess so." Ryan pondered it. "Is that how you feel?"

Cary was silent for a long moment that stretched out in the darkness. "Yes," he rasped. Clearing his throat, he added, "But I didn't want to admit it. I was afraid."

Ryan pressed a kiss to Cary's chest and held him tightly. "You don't have to be afraid anymore. It's okay. I promise."

"It wouldn't bother you if I'm bi?"

"I've never considered it until right this

second, but…no." Ryan propped his chin on Cary's ribs and met his gaze. "I haven't been with a guy who was bisexual before. At least not that I know of."

Cary shrugged awkwardly. "I know it must seem weird to you."

"No, it's just different. There's nothing wrong with being bi. Obviously. Plenty of people are. Probably more than want to admit it, or who are afraid to, like you were. As long as you want to be with me, why should it matter? It's the way you are. And I want you." It was pathetically needy, but he had to whisper, "You want me too? Right?"

Cary ran his fingertip over Ryan's lips. "All the time. In every way. I've never felt like this about anyone."

Ryan sighed in relief. "I want to kiss you," he blurted.

A furrow appeared between Cary's brows. "Okay." He laughed softly. "I'm right here. Have at it."

"No, I mean I want to kiss you on New Year's Eve. I want to tell my family that we're together. I don't want to hide it. That was a stupid idea."

Cary was silent for a long moment. "Okay. Yeah. We can trust them."

Any lingering uneasiness flared into full-on

panic and Ryan tensed from head to toe. "But it's not like we're going to be a secret if we're together. I'm out of the closet, Cary. I'm not going back in."

"I'm not asking you to!" Cary lowered his voice again. "I just want a little time to figure out who I am before I tell the world."

Ryan sat up, almost grazing his head on the sloped ceiling. "So what does that mean? Up here you're my lover, and back in LA we're just friends again? What happens in Canada stays in Canada?"

"That's not what I said." Cary clenched his jaw. "You don't understand. It's easy for you. Your family loves you the way you are. My family won't be like that. And can you imagine if the tabloids got a hold of it? I'm up for the new Michael Bay movie, and I can't afford bad publicity right now."

"Oh, so being my boyfriend would be bad PR? Thanks." Ryan's temper flared white-hot, and he clambered out of bed and jerked on his pajamas. A voice told him to calm down and not let this spin out of control, but it was lost in a flurry of hurt and fear. "I guess I'm good enough to fuck, but not date."

"That's not what I meant! I just want some time to figure things out. The public doesn't even know I broke up with Amanda yet. My parents don't know. I can't get off the plane at LAX holding hands with you."

"Fine. Maybe we should just stop all this until you decide what you want." Ryan crossed his arms and took a ragged breath. He wanted to shout it from the rooftops that he was in love with Cary—because he was, without a shadow of a doubt—and it hurt more than he thought possible that Cary wanted to wait, no matter how logical or understandable it might be.

Cary threw back the duvet and stalked over to the other side of the room. "Fine. If that's the way you want it."

"The way *I* want it?" Ryan's voice echoed too loudly in the stillness, and he winced.

"Well, if you want to stop, then we'll stop." Cary tugged on his pajamas and climbed into bed. He turned on his side and faced the wall.

After a few moments of impotent pacing, Ryan got back in his own bed. The sheets smelled of Cary, and he could still taste him on his tongue. As Ryan willed sleep to come, he blinked back tears and wondered how things had managed to get so messed up, so quickly.

Chapter Six

"GOOD AFTERNOON!" MAUREEN called out.

"Ha-ha." Ryan shuffled into the kitchen. "It's not even eleven. Besides, I'm on West Coast time."

"You've been here more than a week! And by that logic, Cary's on West Coast time, but he's been out with your father and Tony for hours. We're not going to have room in the freezer for all these bloody fish." She stood at the counter, cleaning the latest batch and separating them into freezer bags with an affectionate smile. "But it makes him happy."

"Mom…" Ryan wasn't sure what he could even ask. He'd woken with his stomach in knots, hating himself for fighting with Cary.

"Hmm?" She expertly filleted the fish, removing the bones and tossing them aside.

"Nothing. So fish for Boxing Day dinner?"

"Not on your life. Crown roast of pork, thank you very much."

"Gran! Are you ready to go yet?" Amy barreled into the kitchen.

Ryan tickled Amy. "Where are you off to?"

She giggled. "We're going to the Morgan's down the road to play. If Gran will ever finish."

"Gran will finish *you* if you keep talking like that," Lisa admonished. "You want to come along, Ryan? Greg and Kathy are up with the kids. Kids can play and we can have a nice grown-up lunch. Dad and Tony—"

"Are right here," Tony replied as he pushed open the front door. "We've worked up an appetite. Jack's waiting in the truck, so we'd better get moving, babe."

Ryan craned his neck to see beyond Tony into the mudroom. His heart was in his throat. "Where's Cary?"

"Still out in the hut. He's really taken to ice fishing."

"You should take him some sandwiches for lunch." Maureen washed her hands and wiped them on her apron. "He seems a little out of sorts today." She raised an eyebrow. "As do you."

Ryan busied himself with opening the fridge and poking around. "Huh? We're fine."

"Mmm-hmm."

Shrugging, he took a swig of juice from the container. "We're fine, Mom."

She sighed as she left the kitchen. "There's leftover turkey on the top shelf, and that sourdough bread you like is on the counter. And use a glass!"

Ryan concentrated on making sandwiches as the rest of the family got ready to go in a flurry of activity. Once the door shut behind them, he took a deep breath. *Okay. I can do this. Maybe it won't be so bad if we talk.*

The walk out to the fishing hut felt like it took a hundred years. The cloud cover that had brought a fresh foot of snow on Christmas had dissipated, and the sun was bright overhead. The wind whistled, and Ryan realized he'd neglected to bring his gloves. He clutched the lunch bag tightly with numb fingers, his stomach churning.

When he pushed open the door to the hut, his breath caught in his throat. In the lantern light, Cary was beautiful, his hair golden and cheeks ruddy, his lips a deep red. He met Ryan's gaze.

"Hi."

"Hi." Ryan closed the door behind him. It was fairly warm inside, but the fire was getting low. "I brought lunch. Thought you might be hungry."

"Oh. Thanks."

It was unbearably awkward, and Ryan hand-ed Cary the bag and busied himself stoking the fire. Once he was finished, Ryan hovered by the fishing hole. "I can…if you want to be alone…"

"No, I should go. It's your…hut." He reeled in his line.

"I don't even like fishing. It's cool, you should stay."

"I need to call the airline anyway."

"Oh. You haven't done that yet?" Hope flickered to life.

Cary zipped up his parka. "Sorry. Your dad wanted me to come fishing. But I'll call now. I should go back to Toronto either way. I'm sure I can get a room by the airport even if I can't fly out for a couple of days. I've already imposed too much."

Ryan inhaled sharply. "Would you stop with the martyr routine already?"

"Whatever. Clearly you want me to leave."

"That's not what I said! Would you just—"

But Cary was gone, the hut door slamming in his wake. Blowing out a long breath, Ryan rolled his shoulders. They were both lashing out, and he wasn't even sure why. He slowly counted to ten silently and then followed Cary outside.

Cary wasn't there.

Blinking in the glare of the sun, Ryan held up a hand to shield his eyes as he looked over the expanse of ice between the hut and the cottage up on the hill. He saw movement to the left, and his stomach clenched. Instead of walking the way they'd come across the main part of the bay, Cary was taking a shortcut by a tiny inlet.

They called it the narrows, and in the summer boats had to lift their motors while passing through. With the falling water levels in Georgian Bay, soon it would be little more than rock, with the pond beyond it dried out.

"Cary!" His cry echoed in the winter stillness, and Ryan raced after him, boots sliding.

Cary stopped, but even as he turned, an ominous *crack* filled the air, and he just *disappeared*. Ryan's lungs burned as he ran, blood rushing in his ears. He battled the panic, and a voice reminded him that he wouldn't be any good to Cary if he fell in too.

As Ryan reached the narrows, he dropped down to his stomach to spread out his weight and slithered closer to the jagged hole. "Cary!"

The ice creaked as he got closer, but he dragged himself on. When he came within an arm's length, he met Cary's wide-eyed stare. Cary's face was barely out of the water, and his normally tanned skin was frighteningly pale. He made horrible gasping noises as he clutched at the sharp edges of the ice.

Fingers sliding, Ryan couldn't get any purchase. He unwrapped his woolen scarf and tossed it toward the hole. It stuck to the wet ice, and Ryan used it to inch forward. "Grab the end!"

Still gasping, Cary reached out.

"It's okay. I've got you."

For a moment that lasted a lifetime, Cary's head disappeared below the black surface.

"No!" Praying the ice would hold, Ryan squirmed closer to the hole and plunged his hand into it. The cold took his breath away, but he was able to catch Cary's hair. His fingers were hopelessly numb, but he forced his body to follow his commands and yank Cary back above the water.

Crack.

Another fissure in the ice appeared beside him. Ryan focused on Cary. "It's okay. Hold on to my scarf as tight as you can."

With trembling arms, Cary did as he was told, and Ryan backed up on his belly, knowing the ice around the hole wouldn't hold both of them. It fractured farther as he tried to drag Cary to safety, but he moved back, inch by inch, until finally, arms burning, he was able to pull Cary onto solid ice.

He reached for Cary's arm and dragged him along, not risking getting back on his feet until he knew the ice would be thick enough to hold them. When he was able to kneel, he drew Cary into his arms, gripping him tightly.

"It's okay. You're okay. Can you stand? We have to get you inside."

Jerkily, Cary nodded, and Ryan wrapped an arm around his back. They struggled to find their footing on the ice and plodded slowly toward the shore. Ryan's whole body felt numb and stiff—so he could only imagine how Cary felt.

Once they were back on solid ground, it took precious minutes to climb the stairs leading up to the cottage. Cary's body didn't want to bend, and he finally started shivering, which Ryan took as a good sign.

"Come on. You're a Portigan warrior. You can do it." Ryan's voice sounded strained and frightened to his ears.

Cary might have been trying to smile, but it was a grimace instead. Still, he managed to move a little faster, and they made it to the top of the stairs with Ryan pushing and pulling. The cottage had never looked so welcoming as Ryan maneuvered Cary inside the mudroom and yanked off their boots and jackets.

The fire had burned out, but it still felt

wonderfully warm in the living room. Cary swayed on his feet, and Ryan gripped him as he peeled off Cary's wet clothing. After throwing down a blanket in front of the fireplace, Ryan eased Cary down and rubbed his icy flesh. The hospital was an hour away, and he needed to get Cary warm now.

He knew the best thing for hypothermia was body heat, so Ryan stripped off his clothing and stretched out on top of Cary, his hands roaming. Cary shuddered helplessly, but after some of the longest minutes of Ryan's life, began to warm up.

"You're okay now." Ryan murmured as he stroked Cary's body. "I've got you." He examined Cary's body for signs of frostbite, but found nothing.

With jerky movements, Cary wrapped his arms around Ryan's back. Ryan stilled his movement, and they held each other until their ragged breathing slowed. Ryan hadn't realized how fast his pulse was racing until it returned to normal. He buried his face in Cary's neck and pressed kisses to the damp skin.

"I don't ever want to lose you," he whispered.

"Ry." Cary's voice was wrecked.

Ryan struggled to keep his voice steady. "I'm sorry."

"Me too." Cary's fingers tightened on Ryan's back.

Ryan wasn't sure how long they stayed in each other's arms. Finally he pulled himself away—much to Cary's obvious displeasure—to start a fire and grab another blanket from the rocking chair to pull over them.

The fire sparked to life, radiating warmth and flickering light over Cary's still-pale skin. Ryan rubbed Cary's chest. "Feeling better?"

Nodding, Cary closed his eyes. "So tired. It was...I couldn't move. My brain was screaming, but my body couldn't do anything. I thought...I've never been so scared."

"Shh." Ryan kissed Cary's chest and caressed his belly. "You're okay."

"Thanks to you." Cary stroked Ryan's hair.

As they kissed gently, Maureen's voice suddenly rang out from the mudroom. "What a fine mess to come home to. Ryan! Pick up after yourself for bloody once in your life!"

Ryan bolted upright, still sitting tangled in the blankets as Cary groaned. He kept a firm hand on Cary's chest, not wanting Cary to move too soon. "Mom, wait!"

But she was already throwing open the door, and she skidded to a halt just inside the entrance, mouth open. Lisa, Tony and Jack stopped behind her, eyes wide.

"I can explain—" Ryan began.

"Well, this is certainly what we were all hoping for, but a little decorum would be appreciated. This isn't *Hollywood*, Ryan." His mother's face flushed brightly. She called out behind her, "Children! Stay outside for a minute!"

"It's not what it looks like."

"Of course not!" Lisa grinned. "Do explain then, little brother. We're all ears."

"Cary fell through the ice. I had to warm him up and—"

He didn't get a chance to finish in the volley of exclamations. Lisa and Maureen hurried over, all business as they examined Cary, poking and prodding. Ryan could only scurry out of the way with one of the blankets wrapped around him.

"I told you it was too early to be out on the ice!" Maureen scolded her husband.

"It was a foot thick!" Jack ran a hand through his silver hair. "I'm sorry, Cary. Is he all right?"

"Dad, it's not your fault. It's mine. I never told him not to cross at the narrows."

Amid the hubbub, Cary spoke up. "If it was anyone's fault, it was mine. But Ryan knew just what to do."

"How are you feeling, dear?" Maureen held Cary's wrist with one eye on her watch.

"Better. Like I could sleep for a week."

"Of course. Let's get you to bed." She shook her head. "This is why I say stay off the ice! You just never know. You could have both drowned," she muttered.

Holding the blanket awkwardly, Ryan crouched down to help Cary to his feet, keeping his arm around Cary's back. "We're fine, Mom. Really. We just need to rest now."

For a moment, silence stretched out, and they all looked at each other. Tony cleared his throat.

"So…you sure there's nothing else going on? Because Maria's been saying for months that you two have, and I quote, like, amazing chemistry."

It was Ryan's turn to blush. He glanced at Cary, who studied the floor, a telltale dimple in his cheek.

"Ah ha! Finally!" Lisa bounced on her toes. "Told you, Mom."

"It seemed too good to be true! Oh Ryan. Cary's such a lovely young man and we're all thrilled—"

"Um, can we have this conversation when Cary and I aren't naked?" Ryan asked.

"That would probably be best, son." Trying to hide a smile, Jack clapped him on the shoulder as Ryan steered Cary toward the stairs.

"Can we come in yet? It's cold!" Amy cried

out from the mudroom.

His family's laughter rang through the cottage, and as they made their way to the attic, Cary and Ryan chuckled softly. Ryan guided Cary to the guest bed and tucked him in. But Cary reached for him as Ryan backed away.

"Stay. I'm still cold. Need your body. You know, for the warmth."

"I guess if it's a medical necessity, I can't really say no." Ryan couldn't stop grinning as he snuggled in under the covers. "Now sleep."

Cary nuzzled Ryan, kissing him softly, his eyes already shut. "Okay."

THEY WOKE TO the smell of sizzling pork and what Ryan could imagine were crispy roasted potatoes. His stomach growled, and Cary huffed out a laugh, his breath warm on Ryan's chest.

"I think dinner's almost ready," Cary murmured.

"You feel up to it? I'm sure my mom will bring up a tray."

"I think I'm okay." Cary stretched his limbs and turned onto his side, facing Ryan on the narrow bed. "Feel a lot better than I did earlier, that's for sure." His expression darkened. "I'm so sorry. I never meant for you to think that I don't want to be with you."

"Really?" Ryan's heart skipped a beat.

"Really." Cary kissed him tenderly. "I want you more than anyone I've ever known. It's just so new. My head is spinning. Up here it feels like we're in our own secret world. I can't help but be afraid of what will happen when we go back to the real one. I know I shouldn't be. I know I should be stronger."

"No, no." Ryan brushed back Cary's disheveled hair. "You *are* strong. I'm afraid too. Afraid you'll change your mind."

"I won't change my mind." Cary rubbed their noses together. "I want to be with you, Ryan."

"What if we get back and everything's different? And your father pressures you, and Amanda wants you back and—"

"She's the one who told me to come here." Cary drew away, a smile tugging at his lips. "She was always jealous of you. Finally she told me to just man up and admit I was in love with you."

Ryan's breath stuttered, and his voice squeaked embarrassingly. "Love?"

"Duh." Cary smiled and brushed his thumb across Ryan's bottom lip. "Of course I'm in love with you. Have been for a long time. Amanda pushed me to admit it."

"She's not so bad, really."

Laughing, they kissed, mouths opening and tongues twining. When Ryan pulled away a minute later, breathless, he pressed kisses all over Cary's face—cheeks, forehead, chin, the tip of his nose.

His stomach was all butterflies in the best way. "In case it wasn't clear, I love you. I'm sorry I pressured you. I know you need time before we tell the world."

"So you understand? It's not that I don't want to be with you, or that I'm ashamed of you. God, I could never be ashamed of you. You make me want to be a better person. A better man. I'm so proud to be with you. To be wanted by you. But the idea of coming out before I fully understand who I am? It really scares me."

"I don't blame you. I was being selfish. Insecure."

Cary held him tightly. "I'm with you. Being bisexual doesn't change that. You're the only one I want to be with. The only one I want to kiss at midnight when the ball drops. Or on Boxing Day. Whatever the hell that is." His eyes crinkled at the corners.

Ryan's own laughter was like a balm. "It's clearly a day when...I have no idea, but Canadians get the day off work, so it's awesome. Definitely kissworthy."

"Assuming you still want to kiss me, that is."

Ryan felt as though his body was filling with helium and he could just float away. "I guess that would be okay. Maybe we should give it a try. Make sure we have our form down for New Year's."

"Good idea. Rehearsal." Cary cleared his throat and leaned back to mime a clapperboard with his hands. "Scene one, take one. Actually, take two. We kind of messed up on the first take. But I think we've got it now."

Grinning, Ryan pulled Cary back into his arms. "Action!"

Epilogue

"CAN YOU SIGN my magazine, Mr. Holloway?"

Ryan glanced over from where he and the kids played Monopoly on the floor by the glittering tree. This year Tony's niece had joined them for Christmas, and fifteen-year-old Maria was fairly vibrating, unable to contain her excitement as she held out the latest issue of *Vanity Fair* and a marker pen.

From the couch, Cary smiled and put down his e-reader. "Sure. Come on, sit down. And call me Cary, remember?" He scrawled his autograph in the corner near the headline.

Hollywood Son Cary Holloway Comes Out: Are We Ready for a Bisexual Leading Man?

"And the pictures inside? Ryan signed his."

There was a four-page spread in the magazine of Cary in various poses, along with a candid shot of Cary and Ryan hand in hand at a fall film premiere—their first official event as a couple.

"Is it true that your dad hardly even talks to you anymore?" Maria asked.

Before Ryan could interject, Lisa called out from the kitchen. "Maria. Remember what we said about gossiping?"

"Sorry, Aunt Lisa." Maria appeared genuinely abashed. "Sorry, Cary. I just think it sucks."

"It's okay. I think it sucks too." Cary glanced at Ryan and gave him a tight smile.

Sucks was an understatement, and Ryan had to choke down the anger that bubbled up whenever he thought of how Cary's family had reacted to his coming out. At least his mother seemed to be softening. His father and grandfather were another story, but Cary shrugged it off. Most of the time. Some nights all Ryan could do was hold him, since there were no words.

"Can you sign my DVDs too?" Maria thrust the first two seasons of *Space Academy* at Cary. "I really wish they'd release the show on Blu-ray. Especially now that it got a two-season pickup. Everyone's talking about it. Especially about Stishi. You guys are, like, the best ev."

"And Cary's *soooo cute*," Ethan said, ducking

out of the way as Maria deftly picked up a chestnut from the bowl of nuts on the coffee table and fired it across the room.

"It's true. He is pretty cute," Ryan said. "Glad you agree, Ethan."

"*I* didn't say he's cute!" Ethan protested.

"Sure you did. Besides, he's the cutest. Would you look at those dimples?" Tony added.

As Lisa, Maureen, and Jack chimed in, they all laughed—even Maria, who took five minutes to stop blushing.

Maureen yawned widely. "I think it's time for bed. Santa's on his way, and we all need to stay off the naughty list. Run and get the cookies, Amy."

Even though Amy had expressed some doubts to Ryan that morning that Santa Claus was real, she jumped up and raced to the kitchen.

It was just before midnight when Ryan and Cary sneaked back downstairs. The lights from the tree cast a rainbow glow over the room, and snow drifted down beyond the windows. They plucked the cookies from the mantel and shared the glass of milk in contented silence. Ryan couldn't believe a year had passed already. He pressed their lips together.

"Happy anniversary."

"And merry Christmas," Cary whispered.

Hands clasped, they crept back past the mantel, where a new stocking hung with Cary's name sewn in shimmering gold.

THE END

About the Author

Keira aims for the perfect mix of character, plot, and heat in her M/M romances. She writes everything from swashbuckling pirates to heartwarming holiday escapism. Her fave tropes are enemies to lovers, age gaps, forced proximity, and passionate virgins. Although she loves delicious angst along the way, Keira guarantees happy endings!

Discover more at:
KeiraAndrews.com

www.ingramcontent.com/pod-product-compliance
Lightning Source LLC
Chambersburg PA
CBHW031005210726
48290CB00007B/2480